The

Hotel

Under

Praise for *The Hotel Under the Sand*

"Wow! I read *The Hotel Under the Sand* with delight and joy. It's wonderful, wacky and spooky and serious and FUN. It also strikes me as utterly original (which is quite rare). In fact — although this is something one should always say with some caution — it wouldn't surprise me if it turned out to be a classic and went on down the ages along with *Alice* and *Oz* and the very few others that have become immortal."
—Diana Wynne Jones, author of *Howl's Moving Castle*

"Kage Baker's *The Hotel Under the Sand* will grab you on Page One and never let you go until you finish reading and beg for more. Young Emma is exactly the kind of little girl I wish I'd had for a sister, and would love to have for a daughter. She's smart, brave, and good. Her adventures are wonderful, her companions are amazing, and *The Hotel Under the Sand* will send you back to the bookshop to search for every Kage Baker book you can find."
—Richard A. Lupoff, author of *Marblehead*

"I read it all in one sitting, enjoying the characters and the well-crafted plot very much, and want to read it soon to my granddaughters. Kage Baker used the fantasy structure with a light touch, reassuring but exciting, and the Wenlocke itself is a wonderful creation. Baker writes well without writing down to her young audience, in fact, she invites them to stretch and reach."
—Cecilia Holland, author of *Until the Sun Falls*

Praise for Kage Baker

"She's an edgy, funny, complex, ambitious writer with the mysterious, true gift of story-telling."
—Ursula K. Le Guin, author of *A Wizard of Earthsea*

"Kage Baker has a very good fantasy career in front of her.... Her style is infused with a subtle humor that had me chuckling.... She kept turning me in directions that I hadn't expected."
—Anne McCaffrey, author of *Dragonsinger* and *Dragonsong*

"Eccentric and often very funny.... Baker piles on such delights for anyone who wants more from fantasy than an epic journey to battle evil."
—*Denver Post*

"A fresh, audacious, ambitious new voice, wry, jazzy, irreverent, sharp as a razor, full of daring, dash and élan, sometimes surprisingly lyrical. She is also one hell of a storyteller. If you're reading something by Kage Baker, fasten your seat belt — you're in for a wild ride."
—Gardner Dozois, editor of *The Year's Best Science Fiction*

"An unusual mix of mortals, all-too-fallible immortals, a generous dollop of antic wit..." —*San Francisco Chronicle*

"Ms. Baker is the best thing to happen to modern science fiction since Connie Willis or Dan Simmons. She mixes adventure, history and societal concerns in just the right amount, creating an action-packed but thoughtful read." —*Dallas News*

"Historical detail and fast-paced action with a good dose of ironic wit and a dollop of bittersweet romance." —*Library Journal*

"If there's a better time-travel series out there, go find it."
—*Kirkus*, starred review

"Listen closely, and perhaps you will hear the collective sigh of delight from intelligent lovers of fantasy the world over. —*Booklist*

"Wise, sad, sometimes wildly funny — no Company fan will want to miss Baker's rousing, astonishing conclusion." —*Kirkus*, starred review

The Hotel Under

The Hotel Under the Sand

∾ Kage Baker ∾

Illustrations by
Stephanie Pui-Mun Law

Tachyon Publications

The Hotel Under the Sand
Kage Baker
Copyright © 2009 by Kage Baker

Interior design & composition
by John Coulthart
Cover design by Ann Monn
Interior illustrations
by Stephanie Pui-Mun Law

Tachyon Publications
1459 18th Street #139
San Francisco, CA 94107
(415) 285-5615

www.tachyonpublications.com
tachyon@tachyonpublications.com

Series Editor: Jacob Weisman
ISBN 13: 978-1-892391-89-6
ISBN 10: 1-892391-89-9

Printed in the United States
of America by Worzalla
First Edition: 2009

9 8 7 6 5 4 3 2 1

THE GRAND

FOR EMMA ROSE
So blessed with brains, heart and courage,
she needs no wizard.

WENLOCKE

Contents

EMMA

CLEVERNESS AND BRAVERY are absolutely necessary for good adventures.

Emma was a little girl both clever and brave, and destined — so you might think — to do well in any adventure that came her way. But the first adventure Emma had was dreadful.

One day a storm came and swept away everything that Emma had, and everything that Emma knew. When it had done all that, it swept away Emma too.

It might have been a storm with black winds, with thunder and lightning and rising waves. It might have been a storm with terrible anger and policemen coming to the door, and strangers, hospitals, courtrooms, and nightmares. It might have been a storm with soldiers, and fire, and hiding in cellars listening to shooting overhead. There are different kinds of storms.

But Emma faced the storm that swept over her, and found a way to save herself. She kept her head above water, and kept swimming even when she was tired. She didn't think about all the things that might be in the dark. She didn't drift, feeling sorry for herself. When she spotted a floating tree, she pushed herself to swim faster, and soon she caught up to it and was able to climb aboard.

She blew along on the angry water, clinging to a tree trunk, driven by the pitiless wind, but she held tight and kept her wits about her. After a long time she saw land, far away on the horizon.

As she sailed closer, Emma saw a golden wilderness of sand dunes, hills and mountains of bright sand. The wind kicked up plumes of it, whirling into the sky.

Soon she heard breakers crashing on the shore, and knew it was time to watch out. Whump! The tree trunk ran aground and Emma scrambled free, and crawled out of the waves on her hands and knees. The warm sand above the tide line felt nice, so she lay down there and rested awhile. Then she stood up and looked around her.

There was nothing to see but the dunes and the ocean. Emma found herself all alone, with nothing but the dress she had on, in a wilderness of shifting sands.

She wanted to cry, but Emma knew that if she started crying now for everyone and everything she had lost, she would never be able to stop crying. So she dusted herself off instead, and started walking away down the beach to explore. She had no idea where she was, but knew it must be close to where people lived, or had once lived, because she could see a double line of old pier pilings, worn down so far they looked like black broken teeth, stretching out across the low tide flat. And as she looked up and down the beach in both directions, she could see pieces of shipwrecks, littering the beach for miles.

Emma decided to climb up a sand dune. The dunes were quite high — much taller than they had looked from the open sea — and she thought that if she could look in every direction, she might see a town. She climbed and climbed, wading in the hot sand, up a ripple-sided mountain. But when she got to the top, all she could see, stretching away forever under the noonday sun, were more rippled mountains and steep sliding valleys of sand.

"These aren't just sand dunes," said Emma to herself. "These are the Dunes."

She had once owned a book with pictures of the Dunes. It had said that the Dunes were far away, on a wild and lonely seacoast, very hard to find. Very little was known about them. Was there water in the Dunes? Looking at the bright, dry sand, Emma realized that she was very, very thirsty.

As she stood up there in the wind and the sun, wondering what she ought to do, Emma heard a tiny peeping sound. It was just barely there, under the hiss of the wind and the roar of the sea, but it was there. Balancing carefully along the spine of the dune, she walked in the direction from which she supposed the sound was coming. The sound grew clearer, and Emma recognized it for the singing of frogs.

Where there are frogs, there must be water, thought Emma. She hurried along the dune and the sound got louder. She came over the top of the sand-hill, and saw below her a green place where a creek went winding down to the sea. Cattails grew there, and beach myrtles, and dune grass, and blackberry brambles. Emma slid down the high face of the dune and ran to the creek's edge. The peeping of the frogs stopped at once, but Emma could see them now: they were perched all over the blackberry leaves, tiny froglets, green as emeralds and golden bronze, like jewelry scattered between the white flowers and black and red berries.

Emma cupped her hands and drank the clear water. When she had drunk all she wanted, she picked blackberries and ate them hungrily. The frogs hopped away from her hands to leaves farther away, but didn't seem to mind that she was there otherwise.

Now that I have water, thought Emma, *I'd better make myself a house to live in.* So she followed the creek back down to the beach, to where all the old shipwreck debris lay scattered. For the next hour she dragged planks and sheets of tin and fiberglass to the creekside, propping them up and leaning them together to make a sort of hut for herself.

During one trip down to the sea's edge, she saw lots of little

holes in the wet sand, just the shape of keyholes, and here and there a seagull poking its beak into the sand as though it was digging for something. She smiled to herself. Emma had lived beside the sea before, and she knew what the holes meant. *There are clams under those holes,* thought Emma, *and I can dig some out to eat for dinner.*

And that was what she did. When she had finished her house, she dug down with her hands, as the little waves rolled in and splashed her ankles, and caught the big slippery clams that were trying to get away from her by burrowing down deeper into the sand. Soon she had eight of them, like big glassy cobblestones, and she pried them open with a piece of broken boat propeller.

The clams were raw, of course, but Emma was very hungry. *It's just like eating sushi,* she told herself. She ate them all, and they weren't as bad as you would think, but she decided they would have been better if they were cooked.

This made her think about fire. She would have to build a fire before night came, to keep warm and perhaps to signal any passing ships. Emma knew that people sometimes made fire by rubbing two sticks together. She found the driest sticks she could, far up above the tide line, and rubbed two of them together for what seemed like hours, until her hands were tired and she felt like crying; but she couldn't make fire.

At last she threw down the sticks. "I won't cry," Emma told herself. "I'll look around the shipwrecks some more. Maybe I can find a can of gasoline!"

She searched and searched, and actually it was a good thing Emma didn't find any gasoline, because if she had tried to get a fire going with it, it would probably have exploded. But she found something even better. Lying in a heap of broken plywood and seaweed was a plastic cigarette lighter, which had been lying in the sun so long it had faded to white on one side. Emma wondered if it hadn't been ruined by seawater. She held it up close to her face and flicked the wheel. How happy she was to feel a quick burst of heat, and hear the tiny hiss!

So as the long evening shadows began to stretch over the Dunes, Emma made a fire just outside her hut, feeding it carefully at first with dry dune grass and then putting on bigger pieces of drift-wood. For a long time she watched the fire, as the red sun sank down and the purple night fell. The stars came out, and a bright crescent moon hung above the sea and threw a track of silver on the calm water. Emma watched the moon on the water and didn't feel quite so lonely. It was almost as though the moon were a person out there, smiling at her and telling her not to be scared.

She watched the sea, hoping to see the lights of ships. She wondered where she would go, if a ship did rescue her. *I have no place of my own anymore,* she thought, *but maybe I can make one.*

After a while Emma put her head on her arms and slept, listening to the frogs and the soft boom of the surf.

The storm hadn't taken everything she had, after all. It could never take away her brave heart, or her cleverness.

THE BELL CAPTAIN

IN THE MIDDLE of the night, Emma woke up. Her fire had died down to ash and coals, only brightening now and then when the wind swept across the sand, so she was a little cold. She sat up to put a few more sticks on the fire.

The moon had vanished into the sea, but there were seven million white stars lighting up the sky. Emma tilted back her head and stared up at them in amazement. She had never seen so many stars, living in a city, or understood that there really is such a thing as *starlight*. They lit the Dunes with blueness, under the night, and reflected like points of fire on the black night ocean.

Straight above her, the Milky Way trailed across the sky. To the West it went down to the horizon, as though it were smoke from a ship's smokestack. To the East it went all the way down to the top of the high dune. Right where it met the top of the dune, it looked strangely cloudy. Emma saw two stars close together in the cloud, as though they were a pair of eyes looking down at her.

"That's funny," she said to herself. "That cloud looks almost like a person standing there."

But when the two stars seemed to blink, and when the cloudy person began to float down the dune toward her, Emma needed all her bravery not to jump up and run away. Instead, she reached out and took hold of the biggest stick from the fire, and held up its burning end defiantly. She didn't shout. Instead, she just watched the person come nearer and nearer.

The closer it came, the more it began to take on solidness. Emma glimpsed bright brass buttons, and gold braid on a white uniform, and very shiny polished black shoes. A white cap floated on the cloudy head, with a gold badge winking in the firelight. Gradually the rest of the figure took shape, until only the face and hands were a little transparent. The ghost of a young man in the uniform of a bellboy stood just at the edge of her fire, looking at her with a wistful expression.

"Ahem," he said. He had a nice voice. "Er… I don't suppose you have any bags I could carry for you, do you, miss?"

"I'm afraid I don't, no," said Emma, who, in addition to being brave and clever, was also extremely polite.

"Any letters I could take to the post office for you? Any shoes you'd like polished?" said the ghost hopefully.

"I'm sorry, no," said Emma. "I lost my shoes when I was blown here by a storm."

The ghost flinched at the word *storm,* and wrung his hands. For one awful moment Emma thought he might emit a ghastly scream and shoot upward through the air, the way ghosts do in horror movies sometimes. Instead he coughed and stood straight, flicking a bit of sand from the front of his tunic.

"I'm so sorry to hear that, miss," he said. "Very unfortunate thing to happen, yes indeed. What about some room service? Is there anything I can do for you at all?"

He seemed so desperate to please that Emma felt she had to say something, so she said, "Well — I'm a little thirsty. Could you get me a drink of water?"

"Right away, miss!" The ghost smiled radiantly and saluted. Then he appeared to be thinking, and his smile faded a bit. "Of course... I don't know where any glasses are, or the water pitcher, any more."

"You could bring me water in a clamshell," said Emma. She picked up one of the shells she had saved from her dinner, and offered it to the ghost. "There's a creek right over there."

The ghost took the shell from her — she was pleased to see that it didn't fall through his transparent hand — and floated over to the creek, where he filled the shell and came back at once. "Happy to oblige, miss," he said, offering her the shell.

Emma took it from him. "Thank you," she said. She thought

about the time she had stayed in a hotel and said apologetically, "I'm sorry I don't have any money, or I'd give you a nice tip."

"Oh, that's not necessary, miss!" said the ghost, saluting once more. "Service is its own reward, that's my motto!"

He watched her, beaming with pleasure, as she drank. Emma set down the shell. He didn't go away, and she wondered how to ask him what he was doing there without seeming bad-mannered.

"It must be very interesting being a bellboy," she said at last.

"Bell *Captain*," he said proudly. "Bell Captain Winston Oliver Courtland, at your service, miss! And whom do I have the pleasure of serving, miss?"

"I'm Emma Rose," she said.

"Dee-lighted, Miss Emma!" Winston replied. "Can I do anything else for you?"

"You could sit down by the fire," Emma suggested. "Would you like to tell me about yourself?" It was the least rude way she could think of to ask him who he was and what he was doing there, so far from anywhere in the middle of the night.

"Certainly, Miss Emma." Winston sat in midair, as though he were perching on the edge of a chair, and cleared his throat. "Though I'm afraid there's not much to tell about *me*. I was an orphan, you see. Left in a peach crate on the front step of the Courtland Boys' Home. As soon as I was old enough to earn my keep, I was put to work shining shoes."

"Did you run away?" asked Emma.

The ghost looked shocked. "Why, no, Miss Emma. I wouldn't have been so ungrateful as that. Not when the kind people on the Boys' Home Board of Directors had given me a roof over my head and the clothes on my back. I wanted to make them proud of me. I became the best shoeshine boy they had ever seen. And so I got promoted, you see, to one of the really nice shoeshine stalls in the Grand Hotel in town. What a swell place that was! Gold lettering on the door and everything."

Emma thought his story was rather sad, but knew it would be impolite to tell him so.

"And I worked so hard there, that they said I was diligent enough to be promoted again," said Winston, smiling dreamily. Perhaps he looked a little more solid just then, because she could see that he had once had big dark blue eyes and a handsome face.

"What does *diligent* mean?" asked Emma.

"Why, it means being careful, and thorough, and — well — always doing your very best to please," said Winston. "Taking extra pains to do your job right, by gosh. So I became a bellboy, with a blue cap and a nickel-plated badge. And I was such a hard-working bellboy, in no time at all I got transferred to the Empire Hotel in the city. That was an even grander place! Stained-glass windows in the Lobby and all. I got to wear a red cap then, with a silver-plated badge.

"And while I was working there, a great man came to stay at the hotel. His name was Masterman Marquis de Lafayette

Wenlocke the Fifth. He was a brilliant inventor, and as rich as a king. Came from a fine old family. I ran errands for him all summer, just as diligent as I could be, and when the day came to pack his bags, he asked me if I'd like to come out here and work for him."

"Did you say yes?" asked Emma.

"Did I! Why, I just about jumped for joy. You see, he'd been busy all summer, drawing up plans for a great new hotel he was going to build, out here on the coast. It was going to be positively the most spectacular place ever constructed, a marvel of design, with everything up-to-date and first rate. The Ritz, the Savoy, the Waldorf-Astoria — oh, the Grand Wenlocke would have beaten them all hollow!"

"Would have?" said Emma. "Didn't he build it after all?"

Winston didn't answer for a moment. He faded back to transparency, sitting there in midair; his brass buttons lost a little of their gleam. At last a tear ran down his cheek, glittering like stardust.

"Oh, he built it, all right," said Winston, and sighed heavily.

3

The Downfall of the Wenlockes

INSTON THE GHOSTLY Bell Captain wiped away a tear and spoke in a firm voice.

"I may as well tell you the whole truth about Masterman Marquis de Lafayette Wenlocke the Fifth," he said. "He *was* rich as a king, and he *did* come from an old family, but the fact was, his family had a sort of unsavory reputation. They had a castle and some lands in Europe, but nobody knew where they got their money. I heard that one of the Wenlockes had been a Royal Astrologer to some king over there, and another one worked as an alchemist for some fellow named Prince Rudolph.

"But Mr. Wenlocke, he was just as nice a gentleman as you could hope to work for. Nothing stuck-up about him at all!

Even if he did look sort of sinister, with that pointed beard and those black eyes of his.

"And there did used to be some mighty strange characters who came to those parties he threw. He said they were his investors. It wasn't my place to have opinions about them, of course, I just handed around the trays of those funny green cocktails they all drank, and served them those funny little black hors d'oeuvres they liked to eat. 'Winston,' I said to myself, 'these folks are as far above you as the moon, so you just keep your lip buttoned.'"

"So what happened?" Emma asked.

Winston sighed again. "Mr. Wenlocke had decided to build a hotel out here in the Dunes," he said. "People told him he was crazy to build a hotel on the edge of nowhere, in a place no roads led to, miles and miles away from shops or railroad lines. But he told them that people would find ways to get here. In the meantime, he'd build a steamer pier, and bring everything in by steamship."

Emma remembered the double line of pier pilings she'd seen down on the sand at low tide. "Oh! But that must have been a long time ago. The pier's all worn away now."

"It's been more than a hundred years, Miss Emma," said Winston mournfully. Emma shivered at such a spooky thought, and added a few more sticks to her fire.

"Anyway, Mr. Wenlocke wasn't crazy. He knew how to figure the angles! 'Winston,' he said to me, 'What's the worst thing about a holiday by the sea?' Well, I'd never had a holiday by the sea, but it seemed to me there wouldn't be anything bad in one at all, and I told him so.

"'Wrong!' he said to me. 'The worst thing about a holiday by the sea is, *it's never long enough.* The days and the weeks slip by too fast, and before you know it, you're back on the train going home to the sad, dull, grimy old world. But what if you took your holiday at a hotel where time could be *stretched out?*'"

"See, Mr. Wenlocke had invented a way to slow down time! I wasn't nearly smart enough to understand everything he told me, but as near as I can recollect, he had a machine that would sort of project a bubble of slowed-down time around things. He called it a *Temporal Delay Field.*

"He'd designed his hotel so that you could stay there for weeks, or months, or even years, as long as you pleased — but when you left, only a weekend would have passed in the outside world."

"What a good idea," said Emma, remembering how fast summer vacations always went by. "But wouldn't it have gotten boring, staying in one hotel for months and months?"

"Not *this* hotel," said Winston proudly. "It was immense. You should have seen the blueprints! There would have been ever so much for a guest to do. Glassed-in gardens where you could play croquet and a club for the gentlemen, and a theater, and a library, and three big bathing pools! And heaps more."

"But what would people have lived on, all that time?" Emma asked.

"Why, there was a pantry with ten years' worth of canned food," said Winston. "And a wine cellar, and a preserve cellar, and a brand-new Electrical Icehouse to keep things frozen. And everything was powered by Mr. Wenlocke's wonderful invention."

"What was that?" Emma inquired.

Winston leaned forward in the air, looking very serious. "It was a new kind of engine, specially patented. It was the first and only one of its kind in the world. It could run on anything — sand, sunlight, seawater. Now that I come to think of it, I'll bet that's why Mr. Wenlocke decided to build his hotel here! Plenty of everything he needed. If only he'd known…"

Suddenly Winston looked as though he were going to cry. He faded again, and to keep him with her, Emma asked quickly, "And this engine made time slow down?"

"Yes," said Winston, growing a bit more solid. "It ran the electricity, too, and ran all the pumps and the condenser that filled the water cisterns — for the engine produced the purest distilled water when it ran, instead of smoke or ash. Mr. Wenlocke had it all piped into tanks for the hotel's use. That was one of the things advertised on the brochures: Absolutely Clean Drinking Water! I couldn't begin to tell you how it all worked, but it did. It was installed before the hotel was even finished.

"Mr. Wenlocke set himself an opening date — March 22, just at the very beginning of the season. He booked all the rooms months in advance, to the *very* best people, and the builders worked around the clock to get the Grand Wenlocke finished in time. All the furnishings went in, the pantry was stocked with the most expensive delicacies, and all those rich people from Back East and Europe sent their trunks on ahead to be ready when they arrived by steamer. And I was made Bell Captain, and given a white cap and a *gold-plated* badge!

"But no sooner had the last carpenter hammered in the last nail, and the last painter put on the last piece of gold leaf, than an awful catastrophe happened." Winston did begin to cry now, and transparent tears rolled down his transparent cheeks. He gulped back a sob.

"What was it?" Emma hoped he wouldn't get so upset that he'd vanish completely. "Please tell me!"

"It was the Storm of the Equinox," said Winston, in a broken voice. "The fiercest and most terrible storm of the year. Nobody had ever built anything here in the Dunes before, so nobody knew what could happen. It came out of a clear starry sky. One minute everything was calm, and then — it was like an explosion!"

Emma nodded. She knew all about storms.

"The wind rose with a shriek that made your hair stand on end," said Winston. "It beat the sea flat so it looked like dented tin. It tore into the Dunes and sent up columns of sand a half-mile high, and in an instant you couldn't see your hand in front of your face. The moon disappeared. There was nothing outside the windows but flying sand.

"I ran down to the big front lobby, where all the rest of the staff were huddled together. We were the only ones there, you see, because the first guests weren't going to arrive until the next morning. That was where we were when we felt the first shudder, and heard the first awful CREAK."

"What was it?" Emma demanded.

Winston drew out a transparent handkerchief and mopped his streaming eyes. "The storm had begun to drive sand out from under the foundation of the hotel," he said, and blew his nose. "The whole place was tilting. And at the same time, sand was being driven *over* the hotel, so it was being buried! Mr. Wenlocke came running down the stairs from his grand suite, and he used some pretty bad language, I don't mind telling you.

"He shouted for us all to get out, to get to the band pavilion on the steamer pier, and he led the way himself. Everyone ran away through those big double doors... except me."

"Why didn't you go too?"

"Because I thought I ought to stay at my post," said Winston. "I was the Bell Captain, after all. I hadn't got where I was in life by shirking my duty! And... oh, if you'd seen the Grand Wenlocke, you'd know why I stayed. I loved her, from her parquet floors to her coffered ceilings trimmed in gold. She was the finest hotel in the whole world. She was my *home*. My first real home.

"But Fate had other ideas. The wind got so loud the crystal pendants on the lamps shook, and then suddenly the floor pitched from beneath my feet as the hotel went up on end. I went sliding all the way down the marble floor of the Lobby and was catapulted through the front doors into the storm.

"I scrambled to my feet and turned around in time to see the entire hotel sinking like a ship under the waves of sand, disappearing before my eyes. The last sight I saw was her sign, all those hundreds of little electric bulbs spelling out THE GRAND WENLOCKE, still shining away through the darkness as the Dunes engulfed her.

"I shouted, and tried to dive after her. I think I intended to try to dig her out. But the sand blew so fiercely I couldn't see, and then I couldn't breathe, and... I guess I got buried too."

⁕

THE WIND

"THAT'S SO SAD!" said Emma. "Didn't anyone ever try to dig down and find you?"

"I don't think anyone did," said Winston, tucking away his handkerchief. "If Mr. Wenlocke got away alive, he must have been a ruined man; all his money was in that hotel. When he was moving in I helped him carry strongboxes of gold up to his suite, and he told me he'd put them away himself in his hidden safe place.

"And what would he have told all his investors, when the hotel sank? Some of them seemed to be — well, not very nice people. He would probably have had to go away and live incognito somewhere."

At this point Emma noticed that Winston seemed to be fading

again, although he was no longer as upset as he had been. Looking around, she saw that the sky was getting lighter. The long night had ended, and the stars had gone home.

Winston's voice continued, getting softer now: "In all this time, you're the first person I've seen. I thought you were one of the guests, arriving at last. Sometimes I get confused..."

His voice trailed away into silence, and, as Emma watched, Winston began to vanish: first his face and hands, and then his white uniform, and finally there were only the gleaming brass buttons and the winking gold of his badge. Then the first rays of the rising sun touched the high dune, turning everything gold, and she could no longer see where he had been at all.

"At least he wasn't a scary ghost," said Emma to herself.

She got up and added more sticks to her fire, because she knew it's important to keep your fire going when you've been cast away. Then she went to the creek and washed as well as she could without soap or towels. The frogs watched her, and politely hopped from leaf to leaf as she picked blackberries for her breakfast.

It was turning into a bright, clear day, hot as summer but with the tired-looking light of early autumn. Emma remembered what Winston had told her about the Storm of the Equinox coming out of a clear sky. It worried her a little because she was pretty sure that there are two Equinoxes every year, one on the first day of spring and the other on the first day of autumn.

"If this place has such awful weather," she told herself, "I'd better make myself a much safer place to live."

So all that day Emma worked hard, walking up and down the beach, dragging more wreckage to her camp. She dug holes and stuck down tree branches and two-by-fours, making a fence to keep the blowing sand out.

That afternoon she found the best thing of all: half-buried in the rippled sand was an aluminum rowboat. Its stern had broken away, but the rest of it was all in one piece. *This will never float again, but if I can dig it out, I can turn it upside down and sleep under it,* thought Emma. *It will be just like a tent, only stronger.*

She spent the rest of the day digging out the boat with a piece of plank, and then dragging the boat up the beach to her camp. It was awfully heavy, but she just kept thinking of how nicely it would keep the winter rain out. *Besides,* she thought, *if it's heavy, it will be hard for the wind to blow it away.*

So at last Emma set it down by her fire. Night was falling fast, and the smiling moon was already bright. She had just enough time to collect driftwood for her fire and dig a few clams for her supper before it got dark. The clams did taste a lot better when they were baked in the coals, but Emma was so tired she didn't care very much. She just wanted to sleep. So, as soon as she had built up the fire, she crawled under the rowboat, curled up, and closed her eyes.

BOOM!

It seemed only a second or so later that Emma was startled awake by wind roaring as loud as a freight train. She looked out from under the rowboat and saw no moon, no stars, but only her little fire fanned to hot flames by the gust. Sand hissed by, piling up against the fence she had worked so hard to build, forming hills that rose and rose and then collapsed, rushing on over the face of the dune. Her hair whipped about her face, and the sand stung her skin.

Emma ducked back under the rowboat, trying very hard to remain calm.

"As long as I stay in here where I can breathe, I'll be safe," she told herself. "There's no use in running out into the night and getting lost."

So she curled up again, and lay there listening to the sand scouring away at the bottom of the rowboat. But after a while it became dark and hot and stuffy, and Emma realized that the rowboat was being buried by the blowing sand. "Oh, no!" she cried, and got on her hands and knees and pushed upward, bracing her back against the boat.

The rowboat lifted clear of the sand, and cool air came in again. But more sand came blowing in underneath, faster and faster, and it buried her hands and feet. She lifted them free, shaking off the sand. The wind was screaming now, so loud she couldn't even hear the beating of her own heart. Emma realized that if she lifted the boat too high, even as big and heavy as it was, the wind might snatch it away. She was very scared, but she was even more angry.

"No!" she cried. "I didn't live through one storm just so another one could get me!"

She clung tightly to the gunwales of the boat, stubbornly pushing it up every time the sand grew too high. She had to keep at it for what seemed like hours, and she was getting very tired, when suddenly someone was there under the boat with her.

"Hold on, Miss Emma!" shouted Winston. He grabbed hold of the gunwale too, and lifted the boat clear of another few inches of sand. "Be resolute!"

"What does *resolute* mean?" Emma shouted back.

"It means — you won't give up!" said Winston.

"Then I *will* be resolute!" said Emma fiercely, and she pushed against the howling wind with all her strength.

They fought the storm for three whole hours, and it got so loud that they couldn't speak to each other. Emma found it strange that she was alone in the dark with a ghost, but not frightened of him at all.

After a long, long time she noticed that the wind seemed to be dropping at last, and a little gray light could be seen coming in from outside. It seemed to have been a few minutes since they had had to push the boat free of the sand.

"I think you might be safe now, Miss Emma," said Winston. His voice had a funny echoing quality, because Emma's ears were still ringing from the noise of the gale.

"Let's stand up, and lift the boat with us," said Emma. "That way we can see what's going on without getting sand blown in our eyes."

So they stood together, and in the gray light of dawn saw that they were still standing in the oasis of dune grass and blackberry bushes. But it was not in a valley anymore; it was on the edge of a steep-sided bluff of sand.

Suddenly the wind came blustering straight at them. It plucked the boat off their shoulders as though it weighed no more than a straw hat, and tumbled it away behind them, end over end, far away across the trackless waste of sand to the edge of the horizon.

But neither Emma nor Winston noticed.

They were staring in astonishment at what had appeared before them, rising from where the high dune had been. It was a palace of turrets and spires, verandahs and cupolas, scrollwork and gilded weathervanes. In some places it was five stories tall. It was the most beautiful building Emma had ever seen, and brightly burning lights above the fourth-floor balcony spelled out its name:

THE GRAND WENLOCKE

THE GRAND WENLOCKE

"OH, MY GOSH!" cried Winston. He slid down the bluff to the hotel, so excited he didn't remember he was a ghost and could fly. "Oh, *look* at her!"

Emma slid after him, yelling, "But how can the lights still be on, after all this time?"

"Who knows? It's as though no time has passed at all!" cried Winston gleefully. He landed on the great front steps and turned, throwing Emma a snappy salute. "Welcome to the Grand Wenlocke."

Emma reached the bottom of the staircase and looked up at him. His eyes sparkled, and he seemed almost solid as a living person. Cautiously, she put her foot on the first step. It was real and solid too. She climbed the steps, staring up in wonder.

The rising sun lit the gilded weathervanes, cut glass, and carved eaves.

"Why hasn't the wind ever uncovered it before?"

"I don't know why," said Winston. "Unless it had something to do with that fence you put up — perhaps it deflected the wind just right! It must have turned the gusts back on themselves, and dug out the hotel. Thank you, Miss Emma!" Winston bowed and tried to open the big front doors for her, but they would not budge. "What the heck?" he muttered.

Emma walked along the verandah and peered through a window. She saw a big Victorian lobby, with a marble floor and Turkish carpets, and chairs and sofas covered in fancy brocade. Right on the other side of the window was a vase, lying on its side on a tabletop. Its flowers had spilled out, and she could see some scattered on the carpet below. They were big, white, frilly tulips, white cabbage roses, and white delphiniums. They looked as fresh as though they had been picked that morning.

Emma rubbed her eyes and looked harder. Was there a faint blue glow, flickering over everything? She leaned closer to see. Her nose touched the windowpane, and she felt a sparking shock.

"Oh!" She jumped back.

Winston was still struggling with the doors. "I can't think why they won't open," he said. Very carefully, Emma put out one finger and touched the door handle. There was another spark.

"There's electricity all around the walls," she said.

Winston slapped his forehead. "Of course! It must be Mr. Wenlocke's Temporal Delay Field," he said. "Perhaps it's gotten stuck and stopped time in there."

"Maybe you could walk through the wall and unlock it from the inside," Emma suggested.

Winston nodded gamely and tried, but bumped into the solid wall and staggered back. "Well, that won't work," he said. "And I'll bet I know why. That out there — " and he waved a hand at the sea, the sand, and the sky — "is all mist and clouds and confusion. Nothing's solid. But *this* place is real! So you and I — oh, dear. I hope you haven't passed — er..."

He stopped before he said it, but Emma knew what he had been going to say. For a moment she was scared. Then she remembered that the electric sparks had hurt, and she was pretty sure nothing can hurt you when you're dead.

"No, I'm fine," she said. "Can we fix whatever's broken so we can get inside?"

Winston looked around and pointed to the far end of the verandah where there was a big sloping hatch like a cellar door. "The Temporal Difference Engine was under the cellars," he said, "and I don't think the Temporal Field went down past the fruit cellar. Mr. Wenlocke wanted the port wines to be able to age properly. So we ought to be able to get that door open."

Emma ran down the verandah to the door. There was still some sand on it, which fell inside as she tugged on the handle.

She saw that it wasn't very tightly closed, with only a loose catch that had come unfastened. Stepping back, she opened it wide. Emma peered down steep steps just barely visible under all the sand that had drifted in. "I see some old wooden boxes with bottles in them," she said.

"Ah, that would be the port wine," said Winston, coming to her side.

"And a lot of machinery," said Emma.

There was certainly a lot of machinery. As they slid down the steps into the cellar, they saw enormous gears and springs and brass flywheels, as though the whole hotel were built on top of the insides of a giant clock. But nothing moved, because sand had blown into the works and jammed the tremendous mechanism.

"Oh, dear," said Winston, wringing his hands. "I wish I'd been a watchmaker's assistant, instead of a shoeshine boy."

There was a brass plate with writing on it mounted on one of the wheels. Emma brushed sand from it and read aloud:

"M. M. de L. Wenlocke's *Patented New Advanced Practical Temporal Difference Engine.* Self-Winding. Self-Stoking. In The Event of Gears Jamming, Remove Obstruction and Pull Lever to Resume Operation."

Emma looked up at a big red lever on the wall, beneath which was another plate that read: **LEVER**.

"I think we have to clean out all the sand," said Emma. She looked around. In one corner were a broom and a dustpan,

beside the cases of wine. There was what looked like a very large fireplace bellows in another, and no fewer than seven oilcans scattered on the floor, lying where they had fallen when the hotel sank.

So Emma and Winston got to work. First they swept up all the sand and carried it up the steps and dumped it off the verandah. Then they took turns blowing sand from the gears with the bellows. That done, Emma swept up all the sand they had blown loose, while Winston crawled around among the gears and oiled everything.

It took hours, but when all the sand was gone and the brass was gleaming with oil once more, Emma stepped to the lever and took hold of it. She looked at Winston, who took off his cap and crossed his fingers.

"One-two-three-GO!" Emma cried, and pulled the lever.

With a snap and a hum, the *Patented New Advanced Practical Temporal Difference Engine* came back to life. The gears turned, the wheels meshed, the springs went up and down. Winston threw his cap in the air and shouted, "Hurrah! We're back in business!"

He took Emma by the hand and ran with her back up onto the verandah, pausing only to close and latch the cellar door. "No more sand in there!" he said. They came together to the big front doors. Winston put his shoulder to them and pushed hard —

And they swung open. Emma stepped across the threshold of the Grand Wenlocke.

It was even more beautiful from the inside. Emma could see the high painted ceiling, with its sparkling chandelier. The stairs were inlaid wood in different colors and patterns. Graceful old-fashioned settees and comfortable-looking armchairs had drifted down the room to one side, like ice skaters, but they must once have been arranged before the big marble fireplace. Sunlight streamed through high windows of diamond-paned glass and into the little shop across the Lobby, lighting up cases of cigars and sepia-tint postcards.

A Grand Staircase led up to the Mezzanine, and on either side its newel posts were crowned with a pair of golden statues, almost life-size: mer-people, holding up twin seashells that were really electric lamps. There were no clocks anywhere. Above the registration desk a panel was carved with words painted in gold, which read: TIME IS FORGOTTEN HERE.

Emma sniffed the air. It smelled like new wood and fresh paint, and lemon oil, and baking bread, and flowers.

"Oh, dear, these have begun to wilt," said Winston, gathering up the bouquet that had fallen. He took the vase and hurried away through an archway where there was a sign that said **BAR**, and a moment later Emma heard water splashing as he refilled the vase.

"There's quite a lot to do," he called in to her. "I hope you'll excuse me, Miss Emma, but I've got to put things to rights."

"That's all right," said Emma. Winston came out carrying the vase and put it back on the table beside the great front doors. He looked at her, blinking as though he'd just woken up.

"Good lord," he said. "It's only now sinking in. Here I am, back in the Grand Wenlocke, and — and where did you come from? I've never even asked you, have I?"

"You were a little confused," said Emma. "I don't mind. I washed up on the beach."

"Oh! Were you in a shipwreck?"

"No," said Emma, scowling down at the inlaid pattern on the marble floor. She didn't like thinking about what had happened to her. "I was in a bad storm. Can I help you tidy things up?"

"Certainly," said Winston tactfully. "I'll start in the Bar — some bottles have spilled in here, and I can see some books that have fallen off the shelves out in the Smoking Lounge, and, oh, my, I can't imagine what it must be like in the Library — "

"I'll tidy the Library, then," said Emma, because she loved books.

"It's just up the Grand Staircase, to the left," said Winston, pushing one of the sofas back into place. Emma ran up the Grand Staircase to the Mezzanine, her bare feet pattering on the parquet floor, and saw rooms stretching away to both right and left. The first door had a sign above it that said **LIBRARY.**

She opened the door and went in. The Library was a long room, with a big window at its far end that stretched from the floor to the ceiling. It was a stained-glass window depicting a lady in a Greek helmet. There was sky behind the lady, and blue sea, with little stained-glass ships with striped sails on the sea. The lady was holding out a book as though offering it to Emma.

Along either wall were high shelves of books. These were indeed a mess, with big leatherbound volumes spilled off the shelves, flooding around the armchairs and reading tables. So Emma set to work putting them all back, going up and down a ladder on wheels.

She only slowed down once, when she came to the children's section. Many of her favorite books weren't there, of course, because they hadn't been written yet when the Grand Wenlocke sank. Still, she was happy to find *Alice's Adventures in Wonderland* and *The Wonderful Wizard of Oz*. There were strange old books with beautiful gold lettering on their spines, and titles like *The Princess and the Goblins*, *The Water-Babies*, and *The Chatterbox Annual*.

It was tempting to think of stopping and taking a book to one of the big chairs. The chairs were upholstered in leather just the color of caramel, and looked very deep and comfortable. But Emma made herself finish tidying up first. *After all,* she thought, *who knows how long I'll be here? I might have time to read everything!*

The thought made her happier than she had been in days and days. Emma hummed to herself as she ran down the Grand

Staircase again. She noticed the hotel's big front desk and wandered behind it.

There were rows of pigeonholes full of old-fashioned long keys, which she expected to see. But there was also a glass-fronted box covering a big brass lever, which she didn't expect to see. Underneath it, in curly script, were the words *In Case of Pirates, Break Glass.* Emma wondered whether the box used to connect with a police station and whether there had ever really been any pirates in the Dunes.

She stood on tiptoe to see the guestbook. It was open to the first page, snowy white and unmarked, still waiting for a guest to check in. Emma found the old-fashioned wooden pen with its steel point, and had just dipped it in the inkwell to write her name in the book when she heard an unexpected noise.

It was a creaking, and a little pattering clicking, and a heavy footstep. It wasn't coming from the Bar, where she could hear Winston sweeping up broken glass. It was coming from the opposite direction.

Emma turned her head. In the hall leading off to the right of the Lobby, she could see a flight of stairs leading downward. A sign over the stairway said **TO THE KITCHENS**.

Someone, breathing heavily, was coming up the stairs.

THE COOK

EMMA GRIPPED THE pen until her knuckles were white, but she did not scream. She watched the stairway, as the noises grew louder, and in a moment she saw who had been making them.

It was a middle-aged lady, rather stout, with a round red face. She wore long skirts and a shawl over her shoulders, which wasn't surprising to Emma. Her hair was fastened up with long pins in an old-fashioned way, which wasn't surprising either. But the black eye-patch she wore *was* a bit startling. A little dachshund scrambled up the stairs after her.

"I think something must have happened, Shorty," she was saying to the little dog. "Where has everyone gone?"

The dachshund spotted Emma and ran forward, barking

ferociously. The lady peered at Emma with her one eye.

"Behave yourself, Shorty, it's only a child," she said. "Hello? What are you doing there, child?"

Winston, who had heard the barking, came running in with the broom and dustpan. "Mrs. Beet!" he exclaimed. "I thought you got out with everyone else! Did you die too?"

"I *beg* your pardon?" Mrs. Beet's face paled to a salmon pink. "I never! I was working late in the Kitchens, to get ready for today. Just settled down to put my feet up for a moment, after I put the last loaves of bread in the oven. And I suppose I, er, must have dozed off. Had the most horrid dreams that the bread was burning. Couldn't seem to wake up for ages."

"It *was* ages, I'm afraid," said Emma. "You must have been frozen in time with the hotel!"

"Frozen in time? Whatever do you mean, child?" said Mrs. Beet.

"Well..." Emma wondered what was the best way to break the news. "Your bread's been in the oven for about a hundred years. But at least it didn't burn."

"What!"

"Perhaps you'd better sit down, Mrs. Beet," said Winston tactfully. "We need to explain a few things."

Poor Mrs. Beet! When everything had been explained to her, she was so shocked that she became quite faint, and in a feeble voice begged Winston to fetch her a drink of rum from the Bar.

He kindly brought it for her, and in no time it restored her natural color, which was a delicate shade somewhere between brick red and boiled lobster.

"Dear, dear, what a dreadful thing!" she said, looking sadly at her empty glass. "I've been marooned in time! This is just the sort of thing that keeps happening to me!"

"It does?" said Emma.

"Yes," said Mrs. Beet, waving her empty glass until Winston got the hint and refilled it for her. "I've had a most unusual life, you know."

"I guess you must have," said Emma, trying not to stare at her eye patch.

"It didn't start out that way," said Mrs. Beet.

"Were you an orphan, like Winston?" Emma asked.

"What? Why, no. There were the most appalling crowds of babies in my family, and not enough food to go around. So when I was a little girl, I was put into service. I became an under-back-stairs chambermaid for a rich family with a lot of spoiled children. I scrubbed the little spaces between the stair railings, and crawled under furniture to dust the back legs, and other things small hands were needed for. I used to sneak into the nursery at night, when the children of the family were asleep, and play with their toys."

"Did they mind?" said Emma.

"I suppose they would have, if they'd ever noticed. But they were given new toys so often they never even looked at most of them. I thought it was very unfair, and I detested those children. I detested being an under-back-stairs chambermaid, too," said Mrs. Beet.

"Now, the Cook in that household was a very important person. She was a good Cook, and knew lots of secret recipes. The master and mistress of the house gave her all sorts of things to keep her from leaving and going to cook for somebody else: holidays, her own room, oodles of money. It seemed to me that it would be much better to be a Cook than a Maid, for a Maid simply spends her life cleaning other people's houses, and what does that get her?"

"A nice, clean house," said Winston.

"But it didn't get *me* a nice clean house," said Mrs. Beet. "It was my master's house, after all, not mine. I resolved to become a Cook too, to change my lot in life. I made myself useful in the kitchen by crawling under the stove to find dropped jar-lids that rolled back there. I did tedious tasks for the Cook, like pitting cherries and shelling peas. By the time I was eight I could make a white sauce without any lumps in it; by the time I was nine, I could steam a pudding. The Cook was so grateful for my help, she taught me some of her secret recipes.

"And then the master and mistress of the house and all their unpleasant children went for a holiday to the seaside. One night, most unexpectedly, pirates came ashore and broke into their lodging-house and carried them all off as prisoners," said Mrs. Beet, smiling fondly at the memory. "So we servants were all given our notice. I pretended to be older than I was and answered an advertisement for a merchant ship that needed a cook on board. They didn't want to hire a lady, but I made them a Spotted Dog Pudding, which all sailors love. They liked it so well I became Cook on the *Flaming Disaster*."

"Did you enjoy it?" asked Emma.

"Oh, pretty well," said Mrs. Beet. "I got to visit foreign countries and see the sights, you know. Had lots of unusual adventures. Mostly good ones, though there were storms, to be sure, and giant squid, and the *Flying Dutchman*, which was a great nuisance. I had to kill a mad elephant with a skillet once.

"And once I fell in love with a boy ashore, and he was in love with me, but he couldn't bring himself to run away to sea. So he stayed there, and I sailed on, until one day there was a dreadful accident when a Spotted Dog exploded in the galley. A volley of currants put my eye out. It was very painful. The rum sauce got everywhere, causing the *Flaming Disaster* to catch fire and sink. Luckily we all escaped in the lifeboats, but that spoiled my taste for a nautical life."

"I should think so!" said Winston.

"But I had a generous insurance policy on my eye, luckily, so I bought a dog and went on a nice holiday with the money. Walking on the beach one day, I met Mr. Wenlocke. He needed a cook for the kitchens of his new hotel, so he hired me. I don't generally like wealthy folks, but Mr. Wenlocke was a charmer, so he was. And everything went smoothly until *this* dismal occurrence! Whatever shall we do now, Winston? Or, at least, what shall this castaway child and I do? For I suppose you ought to go on up to heaven, if you're dead."

"Aren't you scared that he's a ghost?" asked Emma, who was surprised that Mrs. Beet wasn't more upset.

"Looks all right to me," said Mrs. Beet. "I mean, if I've been marooned in time, a ghost is the least of my problems. Mr. Wenlocke did ask me if I minded working around strange folk!" She laughed and shook her head. "And I've seen stranger folk than Winston, when you come down to it."

"Well, I believe I *am* in heaven," said Winston. "This is just the sort of place I'd want to go, after all. And as for what we'll do, isn't it obvious? We'll do our duties!"

"But the hotel's abandoned and utterly deserted," said Mrs. Beet. "For whom shall I cook?"

"For Miss Emma!" said Winston. "She's the only guest we have, after all."

"Oh, yes, please," said Emma, who had been making friends with Shorty while they talked. "Except I don't have money to pay for anything."

"That's all right, Miss Emma," said Winston. "Complimentary service for castaways! Now, Mrs. Beet, perhaps you'd be so kind as to prepare luncheon? And I'll get to work tidying up around here. The storm made a terrible mess."

"Very good," said Mrs. Beet, standing up. She looked at Emma and frowned thoughtfully. "You might think about a bath and a change of clothes, dearie."

"Oh," said Emma, looking down at her dress, which had been through a storm, slept in, and stained with blackberries, machine oil, and tar from shipwrecks. "But I don't have any other clothes."

"Well, there were all sorts of trunks delivered for the rich guests as was coming to the grand opening," said Mrs. Beet. She chuckled, and her one eye gleamed. "I don't imagine they'll need them now, after a hundred years have gone by! So just you go upstairs and look around in the rooms. I'll wager you'll find yourself something to wear. Give the child a pass key, Winston."

"Dee-lighted," said Winston, and pulled an old-fashioned long key from a pigeonhole behind the registration desk. He presented it to Emma with a bow. "You have your choice of rooms, Miss Emma."

"Thank you very much," said Emma. She tried to remember how little girls curtseyed in the movies, and made a pretty good attempt.

Mrs. Beet went back down to the Kitchens, and Winston hurried off to continue tidying up. Shorty followed Emma as she climbed the wide staircase and set off to explore the hotel.

The upper floors were all carpeted in an interesting blue pattern of scalloped waves, with a beautiful lush pile that felt very nice on

Emma's bare feet. Each door had a fanlight of blue and green glass above it, and a porcelain doorknob like a china egg. At the end of each landing were tall windows of beveled and stained glass. Some of the windows showed ships sailing; some had undersea pictures of fish and seaweed. One showed a mermaid looking out with an enigmatic smile.

On the topmost floor, Emma saw a little narrow flight of stairs leading up to what must be one of the turret rooms. She stepped outside on the fourth-floor verandah and looked up. Yes, there was a round room with a pointed roof like a witch's hat, topped by a weathervane in the shape of a sailing ship. Shorty barked excitedly at a seagull that glided past the verandah, almost at eye level.

"I wonder what's up there?" Emma said to him. She went back in and ran along the corridor to the stairs, and Shorty galloped after her. She peered up.

The stairs led to a small door, with pink roses painted on its porcelain knob. Emma climbed the stairs and tried the pass key in the old-fashioned keyhole. It clicked, turning easily. The door swung open.

Emma picked up Shorty and went in. "Oh!" she cried, "It's a little girl's room!"

There was no way it could be anything else. The carpet, unlike the carpets everywhere else in the hotel, was a deep raspberry pink, and the four-poster bed had a canopy patterned with pink and white roses. The white satin coverlet had roses embroidered on it too. The dresser and other furniture in the room was painted white. The windows that went around the walls had fine views of the sea and the Dunes.

A traveling trunk had been set down at the foot of the bed. It was bound with brass, and had stickers all over it from fine hotels in far-away places. Just above the catch was a brass plate, on which was engraved:

Miss Lucretia Delilah Wenlocke

SETTLING IN

EMMA READ AND re-read the name on the brass plate.

"Maybe Mr. Wenlocke had a little girl," she said. "But she must have grown up a long time ago. I guess it would be all right to open her trunk." Shorty wagged his tail in agreement.

She set him down and threw back the latches, undid the buckles, and opened the trunk. Tucked into its curved lid was a pink leather case. It contained a little girl's brush and comb set in silver, with a matching hand mirror, and a funny sort of long hook with a silver handle.

Emma laid these out carefully on top of the dresser, and lifted the layer of tissue paper that protected the other things in the trunk. The first thing she saw was a white lace parasol, furled up tight. Beside it was a doll — not a baby doll but an elegant lady in Victorian clothes, with a smiling face painted on china. She looked as though she were about to wink at Emma and say something funny. Beside her was a hatbox covered in rose-patterned cloth, which when opened proved to contain a white straw sun hat with trailing pink ribbons and a pink silk rose decorating it. Emma tried it on, and it fit perfectly.

"I wonder how old Lucretia was?" she said aloud. She lifted out the hatbox and set it on the dresser too, and pulled out the other things in the trunk one by one.

There were three dresses of calico, patterned with sprigs of pink flowers, and there were white ruffled aprons that seemed meant to tie on over them. There was a girl's sailor suit all in white, with red and blue trim. Under that was a very fancy pink silk dress with white ruffles. Next were white silk pantaloons and stockings, and two long white nightgowns. Beneath those were a short jacket of white wool and a longer coat of rose wool.

At the bottom of the trunk were two pairs of high-buttoned boots — one white, one black — and a pair of pink dancing slippers that must have been meant to go with the fancy dress.

I wonder if she went to parties? thought Emma. She took out the slippers and almost tried them on, but her feet were so dirty she thought better of it.

There was a tiny door to one side of the bed. Hoping it might be a bathroom, Emma opened it. She found that, indeed, Lucretia had a private bath. It was a tiny one, with barely room to turn around in, but all the porcelain in the room was painted with pink flowers, and the taps and faucets were gold. There was even a bar of pink soap, and a big glass jar full of pink bath salts, and pink fluffy towels.

"Hurrah!" said Emma, punching the air the way Winston had when they'd gotten the Temporal Difference Engine started. She wasted no time in putting the plug in the tub and turning the taps. At first nothing happened, and she was very disappointed. But then, with all sorts of strange gurgles and bangs and whistles, hot water came rushing from somewhere and quickly filled the tub. Shorty growled at the noise. He put his paws on the edge of the tub and peered suspiciously at the plumbing.

Emma had a very nice bath indeed. The bath salts were perfumed.

Afterward, she tried on the clothes. They fit her quite well. She longed to wear the party dress, but settled for one of the calico dresses and aprons instead, since she knew there was more work to do helping Winston tidy up the hotel. The high-buttoned boots were hard to fasten up, until she tried pulling the buttonholes into place with the silver-handled hook, and found that it worked like a charm. Last, she brushed out her wet hair, looking at herself in the hand mirror.

"So there, you stupid old storm," she said, and smiled as she went down to luncheon. Shorty galloped ahead of her, happy to be running.

Back in the Lobby, Emma followed her nose and found a pair of tall swinging doors, above which was a sign that said **DINING ROOM**. Winston was busy in there, picking up candlesticks that had fallen over, and Mrs. Beet was just setting down a big plate of sandwiches.

"Why, how nice you look, dear," she said, focusing her eye on Emma. "Found something in your size, did you? That was lucky, I must say."

Winston came and pulled out a chair for Emma, and handed her a folded napkin when she sat down. "Thank you," said Emma. "Who was Lucretia Delilah Wenlocke?"

"That must be one of the nieces," said Mrs. Beet, sitting down herself and reaching for a sandwich. "Mr. Wenlocke's brother has seven girls. Little minxes, most of 'em. Good heavens!" She took a bite of sandwich and chewed. "I suppose I ought to start using past tense now. They must have all grown up and opened absinthe salons in Paris long ago."

"Ahem," said Winston, in the way that grownups do when other grownups say things children shouldn't hear. "Perhaps we ought to let Miss Emma have her lunch in privacy."

"Oh, why shouldn't I eat up here?" said Mrs. Beet, through a full mouth. "It's not as though the millionaires are going to walk through those doors and throw me out. Have a sandwich, dear." She piled three of them on Emma's plate. "Ham on fresh bread with butter, eh? And some of that fancy foie gras stuff with truffles, too."

"Yum," said Emma, and took a big bite of ham sandwich. It was delicious. "Won't you have some, Winston?"

"Thank you, but I don't seem to need to eat anymore," said Winston. He lifted a pitcher of milk and filled Emma's glass for her. Shorty curled up under Mrs. Beet's chair, putting his nose on his paws.

"Don't you think it's all right that I took the little girl's clothes, Winston?" Emma asked, because he was looking rather sad.

"Oh, I'm sure she wouldn't mind," he said. "I was just remembering poor Mr. Wenlocke. Half the family had booked suites on the fourth floor for the grand opening. They were coming out on a steamship. It would have been a lovely reunion for them."

"With no end of quarreling, you know," said Mrs. Beet, shaking her head. "They didn't get on, the Wenlockes. Let's see, what were the girls' names? There was the eldest, Jezebel; then there was the twins, Livia and Messalina; and one was called Urticaria. A bit odd, she was, if I remember. I heard a rumor she was born with black wings. What was the name of the one that kept the pet snake?"

"AHEM," said Winston.

"No," said Mrs. Beet, taking another bite of her sandwich. "Pandora, that was it!"

"Have you found a room you like, Miss Emma?" said Winston.

"Yes," said Emma, and told them all about the lovely turret room. "Do you think I could stay there?"

"No reason why you shouldn't," said Mrs. Beet, pouring herself a glass of milk. "The hotel's yours now, isn't it? You found it."

"Well, Winston and I found it," said Emma.

"Yes, but he's dead," said Mrs. Beet. "And I'm just a servant. I don't count." She winked broadly, or at least Emma assumed that was what she was doing; it was hard to tell with the eye patch. "But you're a proper little lady, and from what Winston tells me the Grand Wenlocke wouldn't have been uncovered if you hadn't built that fence up on the bluff there. I say the place is yours by right of salvage! I could work for you. Bet we'd make pots of money."

Emma thought about that, and decided she liked the idea. "I wonder if we could open it again, so people could stay here?"

"Why, I expect we could!" said Winston, brightening up. "There's a telegraph station on the Mezzanine. We could send out word that the Grand Wenlocke is back in business! Yes, that's just what we ought to do!"

"Mind you, it's been a hundred years," said Mrs. Beet, doubtfully. "We won't be up-to-date anymore. I reckon they've even sent balloons up to the moon by now."

"It was a space capsule, actually. But people like old-fashioned things," Emma assured her. "I could sit at the big desk and make people sign their names in the book, and give them their room keys. Winston could carry their bags. You could cook for everybody."

"What a capital plan!" said Winston. "Oh, how I'd love to see this place full of happy folks, just as Mr. Wenlocke would have wanted!"

He was so excited by the idea that he ran up to the Mezzanine as soon as luncheon was over, and spent the rest of the long day in the Telegraph Office. Emma helped Mrs. Beet carry the dishes downstairs, and was astonished at how big and echoing the Kitchens were. They were full of cupboards and shelves crammed with every kind of preserved food. The Electrified Icebox alone was the size of a house.

In glass-fronted cabinets against the wall, the hotel china was arranged like crown jewels, ivory service trimmed in gold, with The Grand Wenlocke printed on every plate, saucer, dish, teacup, and napkin ring. There were all sorts of strange utensils besides plain knives, forks, and spoons: marrow-spoons, asparagus tongs, grape scissors, pickle spears, oyster knives. Emma stared, fascinated, and tried to imagine the long-gone millionaires who had needed all these special tools just to eat dinner.

Afterward, Mrs. Beet settled in a comfortable chair and put her feet up, and Shorty curled up in a basket by her chair for a nap. Emma ran back upstairs to the Library. She sat down in one of the big chairs and read *Alice's Adventures in Wonderland* all the way through.

She was especially interested by the part in which the Mad Hatter explained to Alice that Time was a person, and if you kept on good terms with him he'd do whatever you wanted with the clock, including speeding up or slowing down time. Emma was rather pleased to think that, although *Alice* had been written as a nonsense story, parts of it might be true.

After all, Time could be changed around even without a remarkable machine. Emma knew that Daylight Savings Time could drop hours out of a day, or add them. She knew that it was possible to live through the same day twice, if you went to the International Date Line and sailed east across it. Maybe it wasn't impossibly strange, then, to be sitting in a hotel that could slow down time, reading a hundred-year-old book that looked as though it had been printed yesterday.

The long afternoon did creep past, though, and after a while Emma could smell dinner being cooked downstairs. She went down to the Dining Room just as Mrs. Beet carried a big tray in, with Shorty frolicking around her ankles.

"There you are, dear," said Mrs. Beet. "Look what I've made for us! Beef Wellington with new potatoes and asparagus with Hollandaise sauce! And a nice bottle of lemonade for you, with a lovely rum punch for me."

"Thank you! Where's Winston?" asked Emma, sitting down and shaking out her napkin.

"Here," he said, entering through the double doors. He looked dejected. "I feel like such a knucklehead! After all the time I spent up there, tapping out messages to half the papers in the world, I looked out the window and saw that the telegraph lines go into the sand. They must have snapped off when the hotel sank."

"Never mind, love," said Mrs. Beet cheerfully, ladling Hollandaise sauce over Emma's asparagus. "When you set up a high-class establishment, folks will get to hear about it."

That night Emma went to bed in the turret room, curled up snug and safe under the white satin coverlet. Winston gallantly stood at attention outside her door in case she should want anything in the night, for it seemed he didn't need sleep anymore either. She watched the moon shining over the sea and thought how much things had changed for her since the first night she had come to the Dunes. How funny it was, she thought, that she wasn't afraid *because* there was a ghost outside her door, and not the other way around.

She thought for a little while about her life before the storm, and wondered what she'd be doing right now, if the storm had never happened. It cheered her up a little to think that even if things weren't the way they used to be, she was safe and warm and had made new friends.

THE SAILOR

NEXT MORNING EMMA woke up and washed, thinking to herself that she would have to try to find a toothbrush in the hotel shop. She had dressed and was just making the bed when she heard someone say, "Ahem."

It wasn't Winston's voice. It was a lady's voice. Emma looked around quickly, but the only lady in the room was the Victorian doll. Emma walked over and looked at her. "You can't have said *ahem,* can you?" said Emma. "Unless you're a magic doll."

The doll did not reply, but seemed to stare out the window in the direction of the sea. Emma followed her gaze and saw a ship, anchored offshore.

"Oh!" She ran to the window and opened it. Yes, there it was, riding at anchor and moving gently up and down with the swell:

a big, rusty-looking old tugboat. It had no sails, of course, but there was a radio mast above its wheelhouse, flying a black flag. As Emma squinted at it, the wind flapped the flag out straight for a moment. She clearly caught a glimpse of a skull and crossbones.

Lowering her gaze, she saw footprints left by someone who had come up the beach. Only the left-side print was a foot, however. The right print was a small round hole. They led in a straight track over the sand, right up to the hotel, and where they went after that Emma couldn't see, because the edge of the verandah roof got in the way. And at that very moment she heard someone coming up the verandah: *step* thump, *step* thump, *step* thump.

"Oh, my gosh!" said Emma, remembering the glass case in the Lobby, with its warning about pirates. She ran from her room, down the corridor past an astonished Winston, who ran after her yelling, "What's the matter, Miss Emma?"

"We've got pirates!" she yelled back. They ran downstairs together, arriving on the grand staircase just in time to see the front doors open and a man come into the Lobby.

"You stop right there," said Emma, scared and angry. She didn't know what a pirate was doing in the Dunes, but she wasn't about to let him loot and burn her hotel. The man looked up at them, very much surprised.

He was a big middle-aged man wearing a long blue peacoat, open over blue jeans and a red and white striped shirt. One of his legs ended at the knee and had been replaced by a wooden peg leg. One of his eyes was gone, too, and he wore a black patch, but at least it did not look so odd on him as it did on Mrs. Beet. His face was rough and red and whiskery. He wore a dirty white captain's hat, and carried a pickaxe. A green parrot with a red forehead sat on his shoulder.

"You two wouldn't be ghosts, would you?" the man asked, in a deep hoarse voice.

"No, only him," said Emma, pointing to Winston. "You just turn right around and leave again, you pirate!"

Startled, the sailor took off his hat. "Uh… I ain't no pirate, dearie," he said. "Really I ain't!"

"Then how come you have a wooden leg?" Emma demanded.

"Well — uh — a shark bit off me real one, aye," said the sailor. "And I had a nice plastic prosthetic, but it blew off in a hurricane, so I had to fix up a bit o' broomstick to hobble about on until I could afford a new one."

"And how come you have an eye patch?" said Emma.

"I was ashore in China," explained the sailor, "when some kid threw a firecracker, and it blew me eye clear to Japan. Ain't been able to buy no glass eye yet, dearie. They're powerful expensive, by thunder."

"And how come you have a parrot?" said Emma.

"Parrot? What parrot?" The sailor looked about him, and pretended to start in surprise when he saw the parrot on his shoulder. "Why, look at that! Must be a wild bird, dearie, and he just alighted here coincidental-like!"

"Pieces of eight! Pieces of eight!" squawked the parrot.

"Hush, you bloody bird!" muttered the sailor.

"And how come your ship is out there flying the Jolly Roger?" said Emma.

The sailor winced, and twisted his hat in his hand. "Well, uh — that's just a joke, like. A bit o' fun. I'm more what you'd call a *salvager*, dearie. Sure I am."

"What are you planning to do with that pickaxe, then, may

I ask?" said Winston, advancing on him down the stairs. The sailor smiled craftily.

"Why, I was a-planning to salvage this here derelict hotel, matey," he said.

"Well, you can't, because I got here first, and I've already salvaged it," said Emma. "So you just take your pickaxe and go away."

At that moment, there was a rapid patter of little feet and Shorty came rocketing up the stairs from the Kitchens. He saw the sailor and began barking fiercely. Mrs. Beet came up the stairs after him, but stopped still when she saw the sailor.

"Oh, my!" Her eye widened. Her hands fluttered up to her hair, smoothing it and tucking back loose hairpins. "Oh, goodness me, who is this handsome stranger?"

The sailor grinned, showing dreadful cavities in his teeth. "Haar! Captain Ned Doubloon, ma'am, at yer service." He bowed low. A cutlass fell from under his coat and clattered on the marble floor.

Shorty grabbed up the cutlass in his strong little jaws, and ran up to present it to Emma. Emma took the cutlass, feeling much braver, and pointed it at Captain Doubloon.

"Go on," she said firmly. "Go find someplace else to pillage."

"Aw, now, dearie, who said anything about *pillaging?*" said Captain Doubloon. "That ain't my intention in the least. Why, I been a-waiting for this here lovely phantom of the sands to show

herself these fifty years and more."

"I think perhaps you should explain yourself, sir," said Winston.

"To be sure, matey," said Captain Doubloon, rubbing his whiskery chin. He looked around. "That looks like a nice Bar over there. Why don't we all go sit down friendly-like, and if you've a glass of rum for an old sailor, I'll be happy to tell you me story."

9

THE MAP

THEY ALL WENT into the Bar, which was a rather dark room full of model ships and framed prints of sea-battles. Winston went behind the bar and brought out rum for Captain Doubloon and Mrs. Beet, and a bottle of sarsaparilla for Emma. They all sat down at a table. Captain Doubloon began:

"I been a sailor since I was a little lad, and me father afore me, and his father afore him. That was me grandfather, Jack Doubloon. Now, when me granddad was only a cabin boy, he was working on a ship that sailed along this very coast, trading in coconuts and spice from the islands.

"He'd heard tales of a fine big hotel some rich man was a-building here in these Dunes, but he didn't believe 'em. Every sailor knows that the Storm of the Equinox hits pretty hard in these parts. Didn't seem smart-like, if you know what I mean.

"Well, so the Equinox come around that spring, and it were a powerful storm indeed. His ship, that was the old *Tiger's Eye*, was near cast on a lee shore five times that night. Come dawn, the sailors was all so tired they was asleep in the rigging, taking in sail in their dreams.

"Then the lookout, he gave a yell, and young Jack Doubloon he looked to windward and saw something he'd never seen afore: a band pavilion, floating on the open sea, all a-crowded with folks crying and praying and waving their handkerchiefs to be rescued.

"The captain, that was old Howlin' Tom Flintigold, he gave orders to put down a boat to go fetch 'em. Mostly they was pretty little chambermaids in black and white dresses, and young bell-boys with brass buttons, and a night clerk or two. But one of 'em was a tall man with a black beard, proud as the devil, all in fine clothes.

"Well, so they come aboard. The tall man said his name was Wenlocke, and told a sad tale of the Storm of the Equinox sinking his fine big hotel under the Dunes, and blowing his steamer pier to pieces, and washing him and his staff out to sea. He wanted Captain Flintigold to take him to Europe. He promised him gold and jewels from some castle he had.

"But all Mr. Wenlocke had on him to pay for his passage, see, was a gold watch and seal. And Captain Flintigold, he was a hard man. He said the most he'd do for the gold watch and seal was drop Mr. Wenlocke and his staff off at his next port of call, which was San Francisco.

"Mr. Wenlocke, he cursed some mighty strange curses, but there wasn't nothing he could do. He and his staff had to settle down in the hold amongst the coconuts and make themselves as comfortable as they could whilst the *Tiger's Eye* sailed on to San Francisco.

"But Jack Doubloon, he liked Mr. Wenlocke. He never heard such fine cursing in his life as he heard from that man. So he made himself agreeable, smuggling him extra bits of salt horse and hardtack to eat, and they become friendly. Mr. Wenlocke asked for paper and ink, and me granddad stole 'em from the ship's clerk for him, and Mr. Wenlocke used to sit up nights drawing and writing away by the light of a candle.

"When they come to San Francisco, what should they spy lined up all along the waterfront but a dozen lawyers, all a-waiting for poor Mr. Wenlocke with hungry eyes. 'I'm done for,' says Mr. Wenlocke, and he gets ready to jump overboard and drown hisself in the sea.

"'Never fear,' says young Jack Doubloon. 'We'll save you yet.' And as the *Tiger's Eye* docked, a powerful thick fog come down, such as they get in San Francisco. Me granddad, he traded clothes with Mr. Wenlocke, and gave him a knife and a compass. He lowered him in a boat off the port side of the ship, whilst the lawyers was a-coming up the gangplank on the starboard side like sharks on legs.

"Mr. Wenlocke, afore he rowed away into the fog, he said, 'Doubloon, you been a good friend to me. Here's something for your trouble.' And he slipped him a rolled-up bit of paper with writing on it. 'And I wouldn't sail with Captain Flintigold any more, either, if I were you,' he added. Then he bent to the oars and slipped away, and escaped. Where he went, I never heard.

"Well, me granddad were smart as paint, but he never had no schooling, so he couldn't read. He put that piece of paper in his sea-chest, and there it stayed for forty year. Me dad, Roger Doubloon, he couldn't read neither, so he passed the paper on to me without knowing what it was. But he told me the whole story, so he did, including the bit where me granddad left Captain Flintigold and shipped out with somebody else, and heard that the *Tiger's Eye* ran aground off Cape San Martin not three months later.

"Now, I *had* to go to school, what with the law and all, so as soon as I learned to read I looked at that bit of paper and saw it was a map, with directions. It gave the longitude and latitude of where his hotel sunk, so it did, but there was more: a scribble saying as how he had a treasure hid in the hotel, and how to find it.

"And all me life, dearie, I been a-sailing up and down this here coast, every spring and every autumn, waiting for the Storms of the Equinox. 'Some day, Ned,' I said to meself, 'Some day there'll be another almighty *big* storm what'll uncover that there hotel again, and you can go hunt for that treasure, what's rightfully yours on account of Mr. Wenlocke gave your granddad the map to it.'

"So imagine how it breaks me poor heart, ma'am," said Captain Doubloon, turning to Mrs. Beet with tears in his eye, "after a whole lifetime of dreaming, and hoping, and searching — to get here and find all that lovely money's slipped away because somebody else got here first!" He began to sob loudly, pulling out a large spotted handkerchief and holding it to his eye.

"Poor dear," said Mrs. Beet, patting his shoulder sympathetically.

"I suppose in that case he *is* entitled to the treasure," said Winston, looking uncomfortable. "If it was Mr. Wenlocke's wish."

"I guess it would be all right, if he only took the treasure," said Emma.

"Right!" said Captain Doubloon, sticking the handkerchief back in his pocket and leaning forward across the table, his eye bright and hard. "Let's sign articles, dearie. You salvaged this hotel? Well, good for you, says I, but what will you do if another Storm of the Equinox buries her again, eh? There's a powerful lot of sand in these here Dunes."

"That's true," said Emma cautiously. It was a scary idea.

"Now, I been thinking about this for fifty years, and I come up with a plan," said Captain Doubloon. "I got five thousand hollow oil drums in the hold of me ship out there, and five mile of cable chain.

"What I reckoned I'd do was find the treasure, and then rig this hotel with them hollow drums so she'd float, and pull her out of the sand. Then I'd tow her across the sea to a tropical island I knows of. There ain't no Storms of the Equinox to do no harm there, but lots of green palm trees and rich folks as comes on cruise ships wanting a nice place to stay.

"You let me keep me treasure, and you got me solemn word I'll tow yer hotel to that island. Then you'll set up business, and I'll go me own way. Unless you'd like a partner, that is," he added casually, as he took a drink of rum and smacked his lips.

The Treasure Hunt Begins

EMMA THOUGHT HARD about what Captain Doubloon had told her. "It's a good plan," she said at last. "What do you think, Winston?"

Winston looked very hard at Captain Doubloon. "It makes sense," he said. "If Captain Doubloon is an honest sailor."

"Why, I'm as honest as the day is long," Captain Doubloon declared, holding his hand over his heart.

"Pieces of Eight!" screamed the parrot. "Dead men tell no tales!"

Winston narrowed his eyes. "Ladies, I'd like to speak to Captain Doubloon privately for a moment. Would you both be so kind as to step outside the Bar?"

"I'd best be getting breakfast ready, anyway," said Mrs. Beet, as she rose. "I do hope you'll stay to dine with us, Captain. I make the best Eggs Benedict you ever tasted."

"It would be a pleasure, ma'am," said Captain Doubloon.

Emma left too, but she took the cutlass with her, and only went as far as the hotel shop to look for a toothbrush. Having found one, she stuck it in her apron pocket and amused herself by pretending to sword-fight with her shadow in the Lobby. She heard the men talking together in low voices, and then she heard a sort of strangled squawk that didn't sound like the parrot.

When she ran back into the Bar, Captain Doubloon had turned white as a sheet and was trembling slightly. Winston was nowhere to be seen, but a dark cloud shot through with blue lights was whirling in the middle of the floor. Emma gripped the handle of the cutlass tightly, as she caught a glimpse of a frightening face. In another second, though, the cloud brightened and solidified, and then Winston was standing there looking quite ordinary. "What happened?" Emma asked.

"I just showed Captain Doubloon that dead men *do* tell tales," said Winston. He brought the captain another glass of rum. "As well as being able to do other things. And I'm sure he'll be a trustworthy partner now, won't you, sir?"

"Aye aye," croaked Captain Doubloon, and drank down the rum.

But the captain returned to his natural color over breakfast. Mrs. Beet had really outdone herself. She had made Eggs Benedict,

hotcakes, oysters in creole sauce, and plenty of crisp toast with jam. Captain Doubloon ate heartily, and was very gallant indeed in complimenting Mrs. Beet on her cooking. Emma ate heartily too. It was certainly nicer than raw clams.

When the dishes were all cleared away, Captain Doubloon took a roll of yellowed, crumbling paper from inside his coat pocket, and spread it out on the table. "This here is it," he said, "but all the map part shows is where the hotel sank. Once you get *inside* the hotel, it just has these two clues. *'Begin in the Master Suite,'* says the first one. Now, where would that be, I wonder?"

"I can take you there, but you'll have to leave that pickaxe behind," said Winston sternly. "I won't have you tearing up any of Mr. Wenlocke's fine parquet floors!"

So the pickaxe was left outside on the verandah, and Winston led them all (for Mrs. Beet said, "I'm certainly not going to go off and do such a dull thing as washing dishes whilst the rest of you hunt for hidden treasure!") up to the fourth floor of the hotel.

"This was Mr. Wenlocke's Private Suite," Winston said, opening a big black door. They all went through into the room beyond.

It was quite an elegant room, but a little cold. The green and black carpet had swirly patterns that made you dizzy if you looked at them too closely. The heavy mahogany furniture was upholstered in black leather.

There was a larger-than-life-size portrait of a man on one wall. He was dressed all in black, holding up a gold watch as though inviting them to look at the time. He had bold black eyes, and a neat black beard that came to a sharp point. He was smiling. Emma wasn't sure whether she liked his face or not. Shorty certainly didn't like it. He put his tail between his legs and hid behind Mrs. Beet.

"That's Mr. Wenlocke's portrait," said Winston, in a hushed voice. "Really caught his likeness, too."

"That it does," said Mrs. Beet, putting her hand to her heart. "When we opened the door, I thought it was *him* standing there for a moment. Dear me! People said he was quite the magician, you know. You don't suppose he's come back to haunt the place?"

"I don't think so," said Winston. "I guess I'd notice, wouldn't I?"

Captain Doubloon shook his head and shivered. He looked at the bit of paper in his hands. "It says here, *'Brave the jaws of the Green Lion.'* I don't see no green lions in here, and I can't say as I'm sorry."

The parrot gave a long, low laugh.

"Gracious, Shorty, what's got into you?" said Mrs. Beet, picking up Shorty, who had been whining and trembling. Emma looked around the room. At one side, under several tall windows, was a big imposing-looking desk and a bookcase full of strangely bound volumes. She wondered whether one of them might be called *The Green Lion* and went closer to see.

But as she neared the desk, she saw Mr. Wenlocke's writing-stand. It was carved of green stone, and had an inkwell on one side and a pen-stand on the other. Between the two was the figure of a winged lion, five or six inches tall. "Here it is!" she said, and everyone came to see.

"He's got his mouth open," said Emma, going around to the other side of the desk and peering close. Was there a tiny button, there in the back of the lion's mouth? She took the pen from its stand and poked the reverse end as far between the lion's jaws as she could get it. There was a faint *click*. The lion's head rose suddenly, about a quarter of an inch.

As it did so, there was a whirring noise, and both Mrs. Beet and Captain Doubloon yelled. Emma looked up, straight at what seemed to be a real lion bounding toward her! She jumped behind the desk's chair and stared hard at the lion. Emma knew from books she had read that it's never a good idea to seem weak or frightened around a big cat.

Looking hard, she saw the lion stop right before the desk and lift its head for a roar. The roar sounded funny and sort of hollow. Then, suddenly, the lion was back across the room where it had started, and came forward again in the same series of jerky leaps. It was slightly transparent, not in the way that Winston had been, but rather flat.

"Wait a minute," said Emma. "It's a trick."

"So it is," agreed Captain Doubloon, mopping his face with his handkerchief, as the parrot squawked and fluttered uneasily.

"I daresay that's one of Mr. Wenlocke's magical illusions," said Winston, looking around to see what was making the lion appear. "Not only was he an inventor, but he told me he'd learned stage conjuring. Ah! There it is."

High up on a shelf was a black box with a sort of big glass eye on its front, projecting a beam of light across the room. Winston got a stepladder and unhooked some electrical wires in the back. At once the lion vanished. "Yes, that's just what it is: a magic lantern

device. You must have switched it on somehow, Emma."

He set it on the desk, and they could see that the device was nothing more than a box containing a high-powered bulb that focused its light through the glass eye. Between the bulb and the lens was a little rotating wheel on which were eight glass slides, each one containing a photograph of a lion in a different posture, hand-tinted to look real. At the back of the box was a noisemaker on a rotating cylinder, arranged so that it went off every time the eighth slide popped up.

"A silly prank," said Mrs. Beet with a disdainful sniff. "They had strange ideas about what was funny, the Wenlockes did."

"But this don't tell us nothing about where the treasure is," said Captain Doubloon.

"I don't think it's supposed to," said Emma, looking at the little green stone lion on the desk. "I think it's supposed to scare us off."

Cautiously, she tugged at the miniature lion's head and it came off, just like the stopper of a bottle. Rolled up in its neck was another slip of paper. Emma unrolled the paper and read aloud:

"'The Peacock hates to see his black feet;
But when he regards his shining tail,
He sings for joy!'"

"Now, what in blazes does *that* mean?" asked the captain.

Emma looked around the room, searching for a figure of a peacock. There wasn't a peacock to be seen.

Winston snapped his fingers. "I know!" he said. "There's a Peacock Window in the Great Conservatory! Come on, I'll show you."

They all went out into the hall, where Emma noticed it felt much warmer. Shorty turned and barked at Mr. Wenlocke's portrait, once they were safely through the doors.

"Hush, silly boy!" Mrs. Beet scolded. "It's only a painting, after all!"

But Emma thought she heard a man's laughter behind them, a second after the door had closed. She almost went back in, but then decided she'd had enough of the cold dark room.

11

THE PEACOCK AND THE SIREN

INSTON LED THEM down to the third floor and along a corridor until they came to two big doors of sparkling stained glass.

"The Great Conservatory!" said Winston, and opened the doors.

The air was warm and sweet with perfume. It was an indoor garden. One whole wall and a high arched ceiling made of glass glittered in the morning sunlight. Something was throwing rainbows all around the room, which danced on the orange trees in pots, and the flowering vines that twined up the wrought-iron columns. They danced on the hanging baskets of red and purple fuchsias and begonias. They danced on palm trees, and orchids, and big velvety flowers whose names Emma did not know.

Captain Doubloon laughed. "Here's our blooming peacock," he said, pointing up at the big window. There was a stained-glass pattern of a peacock's tail there, blue, green, purple, and gold. The little rainbows everywhere were being thrown by the eyes in the center of each feather, which were set with prisms of cut crystal.

At the bottom of the fan of the tail, instead of a stained-glass bird, there was a life-size figure of a peacock attached. It was made of brass, but had been colored all over with blue enamel to look like the real thing. Its head drooped down, and it was looking at its feet with a sad expression.

"'The Peacock hates to see his black feet;

But when he regards his shining tail,

He sings for joy!'" Emma quoted. "Well, he doesn't look too happy!"

"Anybody got a mirror?" said Mrs. Beet. "We could shine his tail's reflection back at him."

Emma remembered the little hand mirror in her room, and almost ran to fetch it. Then she had an idea.

"Let's try this," she said, and went to the peacock and took hold of its head. She meant to twist it around, for she thought there might be some kind of pivot mechanism in the neck, hidden under the enameled feathers. No sooner had she touched it, however, than it rattled and gave a mechanical kind of cry. The head reared up on its long neck and swayed to and fro. Emma snatched her hand back and stood well away from it.

"Here's another trick to throw off treasure seekers," said Mrs. Beet, as the peacock swayed and struck, making threatening-sounding noises.

"Don't you get pecked, dearie," said Captain Doubloon. "I know how to deal with a mean-spirited bird, so I do." He watched the peacock's movements carefully a moment, and then grabbed its neck and wrung it well around. Now the head seemed to be looking backward at its tail. The peacock's beak sprang open, and a rolled slip of paper poked out.

"There!" Captain Doubloon dusted his hands and gave his parrot a meaningful look. "Just you remember that, next time you think about biting my ear."

"Who's a pretty little bird?" said the parrot, meekly.

"Well, what do you know?" said Winston. "Is it another clue, Emma?"

Emma opened it and read:

" 'Her song beckons sailors,

Her fair skin is cold

And she sees what you seek.' "

"I reckon that's talking about a mermaid," said Captain Doubloon. "Beckoning sailors and all. My dad always used to tell me, 'Neddy, don't you go a-listening to no mermaids, however sweet they sings, or you'll jump overboard and drown, aye.' "

"There's a window with a mermaid on one of the staircase landings," said Emma.

So they hurried up to the landing Emma remembered, and there was the mermaid, still smiling out at them in a cool and mysterious way.

"Why, that mermaid's the image of Miss Atropos," said Mrs. Beet. "Another one of the Wenlocke girls, you know. Except Miss Atropos didn't have a fish tail. I don't *think*," she added doubtfully.

"But what does it mean, about her seeing what we seek?" said Emma. She went up to the window and, standing on tiptoe, peered out through the mermaid's transparent eyes. Nothing to see but the Dunes, stretching away to the horizon. "I hope the treasure isn't out there," she said, and turned around again.

She found herself looking at a part of the mahogany wall paneling opposite the window, a pattern of carved Greek vases and laurel garlands. Was one of the vases sticking out just a little higher than the others?

"Oh! There's what the mermaid sees," exclaimed Emma. She stepped across the hall and touched the carved vase. Yes, it gave a little under her touch, like a push-button. She pressed it.

At once there came a high-pitched whistle, so loud that Shorty immediately put his nose in the air and howled. Emma thought the whistle would stop after a moment, but it didn't. It only got louder, and shriller.

Shorty put his tail between his legs and fled. Shrieking, Captain Doubloon's parrot flew after him. Emma had to clap her hands over her ears, and so did Winston and Mrs. Beet, and finally even Captain Doubloon's ears were affected, though they were used to years of booming foghorns and roaring winter gales.

Gasping, everyone ran back down the hall, and took refuge on the other side of the landing door.

"What on earth is that?" said Mrs. Beet.

"It's a siren," said Emma.

"Ha! Mr. Wenlocke was having his little joke, I reckon," said Captain Doubloon. "Sirens. Mermaids. Same sort of creatures, you see?"

"But what'll we do?" said Winston.

"I read a book of mythological stories once," said Mrs. Beet. "It belonged to those rich children I was telling you about. Heaven knows, *they* never opened their books, so I borrowed it for a good read. There was this fellow named Ulysses, and he had to get by some sirens. They were on a rock in the sea, singing to lure sailors to come close to them, and the rock was surrounded by wrecked ships. To avoid hearing them, he stuffed wax in his ears."

"That doesn't sound very safe," said Emma.

"Unless you had some proper earplugs," said Winston. He snapped his fingers. "Wait a minute! I know the very thing." He turned and ran down to the Lobby. A moment later he came running up again, carrying a small pasteboard box.

"Here we go! There were some in the shop." He read from the label on the box. "'Acme Ear Plugs! Made of Purest Beeswax.

For the Comfort and Convenience of the Traveler. Positively Guaranteed to Block Out All Distressing Noises Such as Snoring, Cats, and Immoderate Neighbors.'"

"I'll try them," said Emma. Winston opened the box and handed her a pair of little wax plugs. She fit them into her ears. At once all sound went away, except for the pounding of her own heartbeat.

Winston looked at her and said something. She supposed he was asking if the plugs worked. She nodded, and then opened the landing door and peered around it.

Now Emma could hear the siren, just a little. She drew a deep breath and ran down the hall. By the time she got to the mermaid window, she could see the dust vibrating in the air and the doors all along the corridor rattling. The sound was beginning to cut through even the earplugs, making them vibrate in her ears, which tickled dreadfully. A glass dome fell from one of the hall lights, narrowly missing her. She reached out and pressed the vase carving again. Instantly, the siren stopped.

A tiny drawer, no more than three inches long, popped out above the vase. Emma reached in with two fingers and found a slip of paper. She pulled out her earplugs and ran back to the others, waving the slip of paper. "Here's the next clue!"

They had to coax Shorty out from under one of the divans in the Lobby, and Captain Doubloon had to go catch his parrot before they were ready to see what the next clue said. Emma read it out:

" 'The Queen of the Moon, on melodious sea
Keeps safe the key
With vain regret and misery.' "

"A key!" said Captain Doubloon. "Well, now we're getting some-wheres. Only, where would we find the Queen of the Moon?"

"What does *melodious* mean?" Emma asked.

"It means musical," said Winston. "And there's only one place Mr. Wenlocke can have meant. Follow me!"

He led them down to the second floor, where above a big set of double doors was painted the word **BALLROOM**.

12

THE SHIP

THEY ALL WENT in and stopped in surprise.

Emma blinked. She seemed to be standing on a flat moonlit sea. Above her was a starry night sky, where little stars winked on and off. Bearing down on her was a big, square-rigged ship all made of silver. It was only one of Mr. Wenlocke's clever illusions, of course.

They were actually standing in a vast, echoing room, empty except for a row of silver chairs along two walls. The bare floor was made of wood, bleached gray and inlaid with ebony ripples. The high windows along one wall had a stained-glass design of white waves and stars. The ceiling was painted to look like the night sky, starred and spangled with electric lights. And the ship...

The ship was painted on the wall, a gigantic mural two storeys high, so cleverly done that Emma felt she could almost hear the wind in its rigging. Only its silver-painted bow was real, projecting into the room ten feet above the dance floor. There was a figurehead on the prow. It was a silver lady, with a crescent moon on her forehead.

"That must be the Queen of the Moon," said Emma, running down the length of the room. The grownups followed more slowly. As she got close, Emma saw that the bow of the ship concealed a balcony, which was reached by a small flight of stairs.

"That was the orchestra gallery," said Winston. "Mr. Wenlocke meant for musicians to go up there and play, so the dancers would have the whole floor for themselves. If we'd ever had a dance here," he added with a sigh.

"Well, we're *going* to have dances some day," said Emma. "You'll see."

"Look at that there ship!" said Captain Doubloon, with his one eye wide. "I'd give me other leg to be able to sail on a fine old clipper like her! I reckon I'll climb up and have a look at that figurehead, eh? Let's see where she's hiding a clue."

"Lay aloft, ye lubbers!" said the parrot. "Take in sail!"

"Well, if we find your treasure, you can buy a big ship," Emma told him, watching as he climbed the stairs. He reached the top and found himself in a triangular space like a church pulpit, only bigger. There was an upright piano there, and room for a small brass band or a string quartet — although a tuba player or cellist might have found it a tight squeeze. The captain went to the front of the gallery, meaning to look down at the Queen of the Moon.

But as he started to lean over, he stopped and stared out into the ballroom. His mouth fell open. Emma, watching him, turned and looked over her shoulder, but saw nothing surprising there.

"What is it, Captain?" said Mrs. Beet.

"Mother!" he shouted, and turned and scrambled down from the gallery, almost slipping as his peg leg hit the smooth floor. He ran forward a little way before he skidded to a stop. He stared around. "Mother?"

"There's nobody else here, Captain," said Emma.

"There couldn't be," he agreed. "But I tell you, when I looked out it seemed as though I was standing in the bow of that clipper and it was real-like, sailing into port. I could see a little cottage on the shore with its door open, and there stood me dear old mother with a pot of clam chowder. She used to make the best clam chowder in the world," he added, and wiped a tear from his eye. "But she's been dead and gone these thirty years. Oh, how I wish I'd written her a letter now and then, when I was away at sea..."

"You poor dear! Perhaps I ought to go up there instead," said Mrs. Beet. She climbed up into the gallery and went to the edge, but stopped there, staring out. "Oh!" she said, as though something hurt her. She put her hand to her heart. "Wait! Please wait for me!"

She climbed down in great haste, and took a few steps out onto the dance floor. There she halted. "Oh…he's gone," she said, and hid her face in her hands.

"Who did you think it was?" inquired Winston.

"Only a boy I knew once," said Mrs. Beet, in a muffled sort of voice. "The one who stayed ashore when I went off to sea. I always meant to come back to him, but I never did."

"I know what's happening," said Emma. "It's another illusion, to protect the treasure. The figurehead must have the next clue, but every time you start to look for it, you think you see something you lost instead, and get distracted."

"I reckon that's it," said Captain Doubloon, pulling out his handkerchief and blowing his nose. "Though I'm blamed if I know how it's being done. That ain't no stage illusion; it's like real magic. Why don't you climb up there and have a go, girlie?"

"I don't think I want to do that," said Emma quietly.

"You ain't scared, are you?"

"No," said Emma. "But I've lost an awful lot. I don't want to see any illusions."

"Very wise, too," said Winston. "I'll give it a try." He walked up the stairs and looked out over the bowsprit. For a moment Emma wondered whether he'd see an illusion too, but he only smiled.

"I thought so. The only thing I ever lost was this hotel, and here she is! And is this the trick?" He bent down and picked up a small box. "It's some sort of machine, with a dial on it. It feels like an alarm clock going off in my hands! Funny, though — I can't hear anything."

"Oh, I know what it is!" said Emma. "I read a book about a phony haunted house once, and some robbers hiding there put in a machine that made a noise, only it was so low people felt it instead of hearing it. It made people imagine things, and scared everyone off." She tried to remember the word. *"Subsonic!* That's what it was called. I'll bet this works the same way. Can you turn it off?"

"There's a switch here," said Winston. "Yes! There. Just like an alarm clock! Now, let's have a look at that figurehead." He leaned over to peer at it. "She's holding something up against her heart," he announced. Mrs. Beet gasped, clutching Shorty.

"Heavens, man, have a care! You don't want to fall."

But it was not Winston who fell.

A shadow flashed past the high windows, as though a very large bird had decided to land outside. Shorty began to bark. They heard a shrill scream, and then a *crash*.

13

MASTERMAN

"SOMETHING JUST HIT the verandah," said Winston. He left the Ballroom at a run, with Emma close behind him. Mrs. Beet and Captain Doubloon followed them. They were not very fast, so Emma and Winston rushed down the Grand Staircase far ahead of them.

Winston got to the doors and pulled them open, preparing to hurry through. Then he froze.

"I — I can't go out again," he said, in a strange voice. Emma wondered what he meant, but had no time to ask. She ran out past him. She saw a little boy, struggling in the sand at the foot of the verandah steps.

"Help me out of this, you!" cried the boy, in an angry voice.

"You don't have to be rude," said Emma, but she went down the stairs at once.

The boy was tangled in a contraption of snapped metal struts and leather straps that looked as though it had been made from a pair of men's belts and an old umbrella. It had apparently fastened the boy to a pair of metal tanks, just like the ones balloon-sellers use to blow up balloons. There were also a lot of tubes and cords, and a billowy confusion of green silk.

Emma wrenched and tore at it until the boy was able to wriggle free. He stood up and almost fell again, he was so unsteady on his legs. Emma had to catch his arm to help him stand.

"Are you all right?" she asked. He pushed up the swim goggles he was wearing and glared at her.

"Of course I'm all right," he said, in a very grown-up voice considering he looked as though he were a couple of years younger than Emma, who was nine. He was a head shorter than she was, too. "What are you doing in my hotel?"

Emma scowled at him. "It's *my* hotel," she said. "Who are you, anyway?"

"Masterman Marquis de Lafayette Wenlocke," he said. "The Eighth."

Winston, still standing in the doorway, gasped. "Who?" he said.

The little boy brushed sand off his jacket. "I am the last of the Wenlockes. You may address me as Master." He folded his arms.

"All you people are trespassing on my property, so you can just leave. Except for you," he added, looking at Winston. "You look like a servant. You can stay."

Mrs. Beet, who had come out on the verandah, said, "He's a Wenlocke, sure enough. Look at him!"

On first glance, Masterman wasn't anything like the man in Mr. Wenlocke's portrait. He was small and pale, with big green eyes that reminded Emma of the eyes of the mermaid. His hair was fair and curled. He had a rather pointed chin, though, and as he smiled, Emma thought he did bear a resemblance to Mr. Wenlocke. Above the left-hand buttons of his uniform tunic was a patch with the words PAVOR NOCTIS MILITARY ACADEMY.

"Where did you come from?" Emma asked him, not very nicely, actually.

"I escaped," said the little boy. "I always knew I would have to, one day, because it was only a matter of time before Uncle Roderick and the lawyers had me murdered. So I built a helium-powered flying machine and flew away to the Dunes."

"Oh, you poor little mite!" said Mrs. Beet, though Shorty in her arms was snarling at the boy. "Are you hurt?"

"Hurt? Me? Don't be ridiculous," said Masterman, putting his nose in the air. He stepped forward, as though he were going to stride up the steps, and promptly fainted.

Emma knew it was wrong, but she couldn't help grinning a

little as she caught him. Mrs. Beet cried out in consternation, and made Captain Doubloon come down the steps and pick him up. A bit grudgingly, Captain Doubloon tossed the boy over his shoulder like a sack of laundry and carried him into the Lobby.

They laid him down on one of the sofas while Winston ran to fetch a glass of water for him.

"He's cold as ice," said Mrs. Beet, throwing her shawl over him, "and he looks as though he hasn't eaten in days. And what was all that about people wanting to murder him? The poor baby!"

Emma felt a slight pang of conscience at having taken an instant dislike to him. So she brought a pillow to prop up Masterman's head while Winston tilted the glass and got him to drink some water. Masterman coughed and sat bolt upright, staring around. Then he lay back, smiling.

"*My* hotel," he said. "It's just as I thought it would be."

"It's Emma's hotel, you little lubber," said Captain Doubloon. "On account of she salvaged it. How'd you even know it'd been found again, eh?"

"I didn't," said Masterman. "I decided I'd come dig it out myself. I built a flying machine and I knew I could build a machine to excavate our hotel, if I could only get to the Dunes. I'm a Wenlocke! I'm a genius at inventing things. All of us Wenlockes are brilliant inventors, except — " and his lip trembled as though he were going to cry — "except that there's only me left. I'm an orphan."

"Out of that whole big family?" said Mrs. Beet, horrified.

"Things were bad for us, after the hotel sank," said Masterman.

"Then who's Uncle Roderick?" said Emma.

"He's not really my uncle," said Masterman with a sneer. "He's just my guardian. He's been plotting to do away with me ever since I was four."

"Is he trying to steal your fortune?" asked Winston.

"Yes, but mostly he just hates me," said Masterman. "So he sent me off to a horrible school, where everyone was mean to me for no reason. He was hoping I would catch my death of cold when the other boys stole my blankets, or starve when the other boys locked me out of the mess hall. And if that didn't work, he was hoping I'd be sent off to fight in a war and get killed."

"A *Wenlocke* fighting in a war!" said Mrs. Beet. "Why, Mr. Wenlocke told me no Wenlocke was ever a soldier; they just sold guns to both sides!"

"But I was smarter than he was," said Masterman smugly. He lay back. "And now I'd like some hot soup and crisp toast, please."

"I've got a nice Tomato Bisque on the range, Master Masterman," said Mrs. Beet, and she hurried down to the Kitchens.

"Can I do anything else for you, sir?" said Winston, wringing his hands. Emma and Captain Doubloon looked at each other.

"You can tell me what this pirate and this girl are doing in my hotel," said Masterman.

"Pirate! What pirate?" said Captain Doubloon. "I'll have you know I'm an honest sailor, with a legally binding claim on the treasure what's hid in this here hotel, as was given to *my* ancestor by *your* ancestor. And that young lady is a castaway with a legally binding salvage claim, on account of it was *her* got the hotel out from under the sand in the first place! We knows our rights, see?"

Masterman listened to all this and he began to stroke his chin, just as though he were practicing stroking a beard to a point.

"I see," he said, when Captain Doubloon had finished. "Well! Here I am, a poor orphan, all alone in the world — and now you tell me I can't even live in my great-grandfather's hotel, because you got here first."

"Oh, no, sir!" said Winston. "I'm sure that's not what he meant!"

"Aw…" Captain Doubloon looked embarrassed. "No, I s'pose not."

"We just mean you have to *share,*" said Emma firmly. "Or we can walk out of here and you can try to run a hotel all by yourself. And what are you going to do when the Storm of the Equinox comes again?"

Masterman turned pale at that, and looked so small and frightened she felt sorry for him. "But I'm not very good at sharing," he said, and started to cry.

"Don't worry," said Emma, patting him on the shoulder. "We'll teach you."

"Look here," said Captain Doubloon in a whisper. "Why don't we get on with hunting for me treasure?"

Unfortunately, sailors don't know how to whisper very well, so everyone heard him. "Oh, oh, you're taking away my treasure too — " sobbed Masterman. "And me a poor little mite at the mercy of wicked uncles and lawyers!"

"Now, Master Masterman, just you cheer up," said Winston. "You'll feel much better about everything once you've had a hot meal. Look, here's Mrs. Beet with your soup and toast, and the toast looks ever so crispy!"

"I'm going for a bit of a walk," muttered Captain Doubloon, as Mrs. Beet came into the Lobby bearing a laden tray. He stumped away down the corridor, and Emma followed him.

"Good thing the brat didn't land in the sea, square in a school of sharks," he said.

"Awk! Walk the plank!" said the parrot. "Splash! Glub glub glub!"

"He would probably talk them into biting each other," said Emma.

"That's true," said Captain Doubloon, and gave a surly laugh. "Well, maybe a smooth talker will come in handy, if we're going to run a fine hotel. But don't you let him talk *you* out of your share, dearie."

After Captain Doubloon had walked off his temper, they went

back to the Lobby. Masterman was very meek and quiet the rest of the afternoon, and said very nice things about Mrs. Beet's cooking when she served them all dinner.

Then they put him to bed in the Master Suite, and though the bedroom there was just as cold and frightening-looking as the office had been, he snuggled down happily in the enormous bed. He curled up like a kitten and went to sleep at once.

Emma went to bed in what she had now decided was definitely *her* room. Captain Doubloon and Mrs. Beet stayed up very late, talking together in the Bar. And faithful Winston went marching back and forth all night between the two children's rooms, to be certain they were safe.

————✳————

14

THE SILVER KEY

WHEN EMMA GOT up the next morning, she looked out all the windows in the turret room to see if there were any new pirate ships anchored offshore, or any other strange aircraft about to crash into the hotel. But she couldn't see any, and Mifficent the doll (for Emma had given her a name) smiled but said nothing.

Masterman came down to breakfast early and surprised everyone. He had seemed like the sort of person who would sleep late. He had not put the military academy uniform back on. Instead he had gone into Mr. Wenlocke's wardrobe, and put on one of his black suits. He had to roll up the cuffs of the long trousers, and the sleeves of the swallowtail coat and shirt, and the scarlet silk waistcoat came down almost to his knees. He looked like a stage magician who had shrunk himself, but he was very proud.

"I'll never wear that uniform again," he announced. "It may be that this is a little big for me, but I'm sure Mrs. Beet can fix it."

Mrs. Beet stopped in the act of serving kippers to Captain Doubloon. Her eye blinked in a nervous kind of way. "Fix your clothes? Oh, dear, Master Masterman, I'm only a Cook! I was never very good at sewing!"

"I can't sew either," said Emma calmly, sprinkling sugar on her oatmeal.

"But who's going to tailor for me?" said Masterman, pouting.

"I'm sorry to say I only know how to sew on buttons, Master Masterman," said Winston. He looked hopefully at Captain Doubloon. "But I do believe all sailors know how to sew. Am I correct, Captain?"

"Aye, matey, you are," said Captain Doubloon, grinning in a way that was not really very nice. "And if his little lordship is a good boy, why, I'll take a hitch in his waistcoat for certain."

"Awk! String him up from the yardarm!" said the parrot.

Masterman ignored them, looking disdainfully at the breakfast table. "Hm! Kippers and oatmeal. How very nice. But I think, dear Mrs. Beet, that I need waffles with real butter, not margarine. And real maple syrup, not that maple-flavored stuff. And a tall glass of cold milk."

"Margarine!" said Mrs. Beet, her eye flashing in indignation. "What sort of cook do you think I am, young man?"

"The very best cook in the whole world," said Masterman, with a smile of sugary sweetness that made him look about four years old, and a limpid gaze. Mrs. Beet's wrath faded. She chuckled, and tousled his hair.

"You do know how to talk to ladies, don't you? Little scamp. I suppose it won't be much trouble to mix up a waffle for you."

"Thank you," said Masterman smugly, as she went back to the Kitchens. Captain Doubloon glared at him.

After breakfast they went to the Ballroom to continue the treasure hunt. Winston climbed back up into the orchestra gallery, and leaned over its edge to look at the Queen of the Moon.

"She's holding a little jar with a lid," said Winston. "It looks like the lid might come off."

"Can you reach it?" said Captain Doubloon.

"No. I expect I'd better go fetch a ladder," said Winston.

But Captain Doubloon leaned down and grabbed Masterman by the scruff of his neck. "No need!" he said. "The lad here will just go aloft."

He hoisted the little boy into the air, as high as his arm would reach. For a moment Masterman just hung there, too surprised to be angry. Then he made a jump and caught hold of the Queen of the Moon, clinging there with his arms around her neck. Holding tight with one hand, he reached for the silver jar with the other. His expression was grimly determined.

As she watched, Emma thought to herself: *He's braver than he looks.* She began to like him, just a little.

Masterman lifted the lid on the jar and reached in. "There's a key!" he exclaimed. "And a piece of paper." He pulled them out triumphantly. "Here I come!"

He let go of the Queen and fell. Captain Doubloon caught him and set him on the floor.

"Bravo, sir!" said Winston, hurrying down from the gallery. "Well done!"

"What's the clue say?" asked Emma.

Masterman unrolled the paper and stared at it a moment. "Oh, I can't read this handwriting," he said, handing the clue to Emma. "It's too messy. *You* try."

I'll bet he can't read very well, thought Emma, but she took the clue and read aloud:

" 'The Red King will tell you himself,

But only the brave and swift

Can get under his guard.' "

"Red King?" said Captain Doubloon. "Sounds like a card game."

Masterman stuck his nose in the air. "That just shows how much you know," he said. "The Red King is the greatest treasure anybody can have. So my great-grandpapa meant that...um... the treasure itself will tell us where it is?"

"Actually, sir," said Winston, trying not to hurt his feelings, "I believe there's a figure of a red king in the Theater."

15

THE RED KING

WINSTON LED THEM from the Grand Ballroom down a flight of stairs, to a pair of doors all painted in red and gold. A smiling mask decorated the right-hand door, and a sad mask decorated the left-hand door.

"Here we go," said Winston, opening the doors wide. "The latest thing in theaters! Suitable for Shakespeare or vaudeville, and not only that — we have one of these newfangled cinematograph screens and projectors!"

"What's a *cinematograph?*" asked Emma and Masterman at the same time.

"Er — you know." Mrs. Beet gestured as though she were turning a crank. "Moving pictures?"

"Ah! Old-time movies, to be sure," said Captain Doubloon.

"Where's this Red King, then?"

They looked around. There were a hundred red velvet seats, and red velvet curtains across the front of the stage, all embroidered with golden laurel leaves. The lighting came from eight carved figures, a little bigger than life-size, along the two walls. Each one held up a candelabrum with little electric bulbs in it. They wore white drapes as though they were supposed to be gods and goddesses from mythology, all except for the third figure on the left-hand side.

"That's the Red King," announced Masterman, and raced down the aisle toward it. Emma followed him closely, and the two children stood staring up at the Red King.

He was dressed in very old-fashioned robes, all in shades of bright red. One hand held up the candelabra, but the other hand held a sword. He had an emblem on his chest, showing a round sun with pointed rays.

"Well?" said Captain Doubloon, puffing for breath as he caught up with the children. "The Red King will tell us hisself? I don't hear him doing no talking."

"Maybe he's got a speaker hidden in him," said Emma.

"The middle of that sun emblem looks an awful lot like a button," observed Mrs. Beet. "What happens if you push it?"

Captain Doubloon reached up, meaning to press the sun on the Red King's chest, but suddenly the arm with the sword swung down. The captain staggered back, narrowly avoiding having his other eye put out by the point of the sword. "Awk! Abandon ship!" screamed the parrot, fluttering away to the safety of one of the theater seats.

"HALT!" roared a scratchy-sounding voice that seemed to come from behind the door. "AWAY, THOU BASEBORN CHURL!"

"Dear heaven!" said Mrs. Beet. "You don't suppose he's got some kind of guard walled up in there, looking after the treasure?"

"No," said Emma. "It sounded more like an old record to me. A recording," she added, for Mrs. Beet looked confused.

"Oh! Like one of Mr. Edison's phonograph cylinders?"

"That's what it must be, all right," said Winston. "Because that was Mr. Wenlocke's voice!" He stepped forward and reached for the emblem on the Red King's chest, but once again the arm with the sword swung out. Winston ducked, but his hat was knocked off. "Gee whiz!"

"WHO DARES TRESPASS ON MY ROYAL DOMAIN?" bellowed the scratchy voice.

"You don't understand," said Masterman. "Notice what he said? 'Baseborn churl'? 'Royal domain'? He means the treasure isn't for just anybody. Only a *special* person, like one of us Wenlockes, can get to it."

"I'll bet you're wrong," said Emma. She stepped close to the Red King, as quickly as she could, so that by the time his sword came swinging down she was behind his arm and out of danger.

She pressed the sun emblem on his chest. The whole round emblem popped out at one side, like a little door opening. Behind it was a keyhole. "Haar!" cried Captain Doubloon. "Where be that key?"

Masterman pulled it from his pocket, sighing sadly, and handed it over to Captain Doubloon. The key went into the lock and turned — and, without a sound, the wall panel beside them slid open.

Cold Hard Cash

EHIND THE PANEL was a room, not much bigger than a broom closet. You could never have fit a broom or a mop in there, though, or even a feather duster. Every inch of space inside was filled with neatly stacked wooden boxes, except for one small shelf containing a little cylinder gramophone.

"*That's* the source of the voice, and those are Mr. Wenlocke's strongboxes!" said Winston. "I recognize them."

"HAAR!" said Captain Doubloon. "Oh, Grandad Doubloon, see what you missed by not learning how to read?"

He grabbed the topmost box and hauled it out. Producing a crowbar from inside his coat (Emma wondered what else he had hidden in there), he wrenched the lid off the box.

Emma was a little disappointed by what was inside. There

were no jewels, no pieces of eight or golden bracelets. She saw only smooth squares of gold, lined up like so many bars of yellow soap. Each one was stamped with the letter W.

"That's not very exciting," said Masterman, frowning. "I always imagined a big chest full of rubies and emeralds. This is just… metal."

"Aye, laddie, but it's negotiable anywhere," gloated Captain Doubloon, pulling out the other boxes one by one. "Better'n credit cards!"

Masterman began to cry quietly in disappointment, but Mrs. Beet took out a handkerchief and blotted his tears. "There, there, dearie, you mustn't mind about the captain getting the nasty old gold. Here, have a ginger biscuit," she said, pulling a cookie from her apron pocket. "Give him a nice kiss, Shorty," she added, and put the little dog in his arms. Shorty wriggled around and licked his face.

"Besides," said Emma, "now Captain Doubloon's going to keep his promise and tow us all away to a nice safe tropical island. Aren't you, Captain?"

"What? Oh — eh — aye, so I will," said Captain Doubloon, who had been scooping up handfuls of gold bars and rubbing them against his face.

"*Awk!* Hoist anchor and sail away!" said the parrot.

"Shut up, bird! To be sure, I'll get right on that, just like I promised. Just as soon as I've loaded all these boxes on board me boat, see?" said Captain Doubloon.

"I think the treasure had better stay where it is," said Winston firmly. "Until the hotel is safely on that island."

"Aye, aye," sighed Captain Doubloon. He put back the gold, though Emma noticed that a couple of bars just sort of accidentally fell into his pocket.

"Oh, Great-Grandfather Wenlocke, if only you could see your poor little impoverished grandchild watching his treasure being taken away by a stranger," said Masterman in a theatrical sort of way, but Captain Doubloon didn't seem to hear him.

Mrs. Beet looked around at them all. Masterman still looked as though he might start crying again, in spite of Shorty's earnest efforts to cheer him up. Emma and Winston were both looking with suspicion at Captain Doubloon, who was doing his best to seem innocent but not succeeding very well.

"Treasure's never as nice as you think it's going to be," Mrs. Beet said sadly. "I know what you all need! A nice plate of sandwiches. Let's go downstairs, shall we, and I'll fix everyone a little lunch."

So they all headed downstairs. They had reached the bottom of the Grand Staircase when Winston shouted, "Oh, my gosh! Look!"

There were people coming up the front steps onto the verandah. They looked very strange, and there were a lot of them.

17

THE GUESTS

WINSTON THREW OPEN the big doors and saluted the strange people. "Welcome to the Grand Wenlocke!" he said. "Er — "

Emma was astonished by the tall couple who stepped into the Lobby. They were extremely thin and dressed all in black; black veils hid their faces. One wore a stovepipe hat and the other wore a wide-brimmed bonnet, so Emma guessed that one was a man and the other was a lady.

They bowed very low and the man said something in a language Emma had never heard before. It sounded like birds twittering. There did seem to be a question mark at the end of it, though.

"I — er — I'm sorry, sir, but I don't understand," said Winston.

The couple stared at him, and then turned slowly and swept the Lobby with a long glance. Their eyes glowed green in the darkness behind their veils.

"Pardon me!" said Masterman, pushing his way from behind Captain Doubloon and Mrs. Beet. He walked up to the strangers, with Shorty cringing in his arms, and he bowed very low. Then he said something to them in what sounded very much like their own language. The couple swayed from side to side and answered him.

"How does he know what they're saying?" Emma asked Winston.

"He's a Wenlocke," said Winston, shrugging. "All the Wenlockes had unusual talents."

Masterman turned to the others and said, "They said they would like to stay here."

"But however did they know the hotel was open at last?" asked Mrs. Beet. "Winston telegraphed the news, but the lines are broken!"

Masterman spoke to the strangers again in their own language, and listened gravely as they replied.

"The lines went into the Dunes, and so the People of the Sands heard the news," he translated. "And they told the Sea People, and *they* told everybody else."

"Well, then, we're in business!" said Winston, saluting. "Please step this way, folks!"

Everything was happening very quickly, but Emma knew what to do. She ran behind the front desk and opened the Guest Register. "Sign in here, please," she said. She dipped the pen in the inkwell and held it out to the thin couple.

They drifted forward. The gentleman put out stick-like fingers and took the pen. As he signed, Emma looked over his shoulder at the door and saw Masterman welcoming in more guests.

The thin gentleman finished signing his name. Emma looked down and saw that he had written *E. FREET*; at least, that looked like what it said, but his handwriting was so spidery it was hard to be sure. Emma smiled her most polite smile and pulled a key from one of the pigeonholes behind the desk, the way she had seen motel clerks do.

"And how long will you be staying?" she remembered to say.

The gentleman held up four skinny black fingers. Four days? Weeks? Months? Emma was about to ask, but then she remembered that it didn't matter at the Grand Wenlocke. Mr. Freet reached into his coat pocket and took out a small bag of black silk. Opening it, he poured a pile of emeralds on the counter, and looked at Emma as though he were asking whether that would do.

Emma poked through the emeralds and selected four of the nicest ones. "That ought to be enough," she said. She handed them the key and said, "Winston, show Mr. and Mrs. Freet to Room 222."

"Right away, Miss Emma!" Winston picked up their luggage
— though all they had were two large hatboxes — and led them
away up the stairs.

The next to sign in were the People of the Sands, robed and
hooded, who rode green camels the size of Labrador Retrievers.
But the camels were much better behaved than dogs, for they sat
down nicely by the potted palms when their masters dismounted,
and neither barked nor tried to jump on anyone. The People of
the Sands took a while to sign in, for they all had very long
names, like *Grittleth-Rides-Like-the-Wind Scouringale*. Even so,
their camels waited patiently.

When the People of the Sands had all been checked in, Emma
looked up at all the other strange people waiting for rooms. Some
of them were even stranger than the Freets and the People of the
Sands. In fact, she was pretty sure she had seen some of them
in illustrations in books about ancient mythology. Emma knew
they were supposed to be imaginary, and yet there they stood in
the hotel lobby, chatting to one another about the weather and
how crowded it was in Paris or St. Kitts this time of year.

Emma decided that if she was running a hotel that had been
frozen in time for a hundred years, and a ghostly bell captain was
helping her, then maybe the guests weren't so strange after all. She
did her best not to look surprised as she checked the others in.

There were several people, very elegantly dressed, with sharp
and haughty faces. They might all have been fashion models.

They talked among themselves about other glamorous hotels they had stayed at, in famous places. They left a glittering dust where they walked, and several times Winston slipped in it as he carried their luggage. They all had names like *Arcturus* and *Cassiopeia* and *Orion*.

Last came some noisy ladies and one very big man, who signed in as *D. Eleutherios & Party*. They wore animal furs tied around themselves, as though they were cave people. They carried picnic hampers that seemed to be mostly full of fruit, and kept dropping leaves and bunches of grapes everywhere. It took a long time to register them, but they didn't seem to mind; they amused themselves by singing and dancing as they waited.

LTHOUGH THEY HADN'T talked it over ahead of time, somehow everyone knew what to do.

Emma checked in the guests, one after another, and Masterman made sure that the guests who had not been checked in yet were seated comfortably in the Lobby. Winston carried all the bags and trunks and showed people to their rooms. Mrs. Beet went down to the Kitchens, of course, and got to work cooking for everybody. Captain Doubloon sidled into the Bar and mixed a big bowl of punch for the guests.

When at last everyone had been checked in, Emma looked in astonishment at the cash box, which now overflowed with strange loot. Besides the emeralds, there were gold and silver coins stamped with pictures of turbaned kings, bottles of rare perfumes, black pearls, filigree chains, bangles set with rubies, a sapphire the size of a tennis ball, and a vial of something pink that was supposed to cure melancholia.

Emma beckoned to Masterman to come see. "I guess you don't have to feel bad about Captain Doubloon getting your old treasure," she told him. "Look at all this new stuff! I think we're going to be all right now."

"Of course we are!" said Masterman smugly, rolling up his sleeves. "This is the Grand Wenlocke, after all. We're all rich as kings now. We can lie around on silk pillows and have servants bring us chocolate!"

"Er — with respect, Master Masterman, we're going to have to work a lot harder than that," said Winston, as he came down the Grand Staircase. "Your great-grandfather knew that running a first-class hotel takes a lot of effort. Who's going to wait on the guests in the Dining Room? Who's going to make their beds and keep the floors swept?"

"You are," said Masterman, looking very surprised even to be asked the question.

Winston shook his head. "I'm in Heaven, so I don't get tired, and I can work all day and all night long. But there's only one of me, you see? And I can't be in two places at once, let alone twenty. Besides me, Mr. Wenlocke had a staff of ten chambermaids and ten bell-boys. And there was a man to serve drinks in the Bar, and there were three kitchen-maids to help poor Mrs. Beet. What are we to do?"

"I know how to make beds," said Emma.

"Good! Then you can be the chambermaid as well as the desk clerk," said Masterman.

"Not all by myself, I won't," said Emma hotly. "You'll have to help me. Two people can make a bed much faster than one."

"But I'm a Wenlocke!" Masterman exclaimed.

"A gentleman would help a lady, sir," said Winston. "And all the Wenlockes were gentlemen, you know. Except for the girls."

"Haar! I'll bet the little lubber don't know how to make a bed, nohow," said Captain Doubloon, stumping in from the Bar.

"That's not true!" cried Masterman. "At the horrible old Academy, I had to make my bed as neat and tight as an empty envelope. I'll show *you!* I bet I can make beds ten times better than a sloppy old sailor."

"Sailors ain't sloppy," said Captain Doubloon. "Sailors is very clean. We keeps everything shipshape!"

"I'm glad to hear that," said Winston. "Because we need someone to do the laundry, and I'm sure you'd be better than anybody else."

"I'll bet he doesn't know how to wash clothes," said Masterman, not very nicely.

"Why, you little — of course I can wash clothes!" blustered Captain Doubloon. "Show me that laundry, by thunder, and you'll have the cleanest bed linens you ever seen!"

"Good!" said Winston happily. "That's settled, then."

So three days went by, or so it seemed — time stretched out so strangely in the Grand Wenlocke that Emma was never sure. If the weather was nice, the morning sunlight seemed to take forever to trickle across the Lobby, and the bright noon light filled up the long halls like slow flood water, while the gold and purple sunsets seemed to last half the night. Dim or foggy weather, on the other hand, just sped by like smoke on the wind.

Emma worked very hard, but it made her happy to see how nice everything looked, and to see the strange guests enjoying themselves. The Freets stayed most of the time in the Conservatory, lying motionless side-by-side on a pair of deck chairs. They seemed to like the perfumes of the flowers.

The People of the Sands found an indoor swimming pool — it had the word **NATATORIUM** over the door in gold letters, but there was only a pool inside, though a very big one. They spent all their time in the water, floating peacefully while the camels paddled to and fro. The beautiful people, on the other hand, spent almost all their time in the Theater, watching movies they had brought. The Theater turned out to have a cabinet full of silent movies by a Mr. Méliès, but the beautiful people preferred to watch their own. Emma peeped in once and saw that the movies just showed the beautiful people themselves, lying on the sand at beaches or wearing evening dress at fancy nightclubs.

Mr. Eleutherios and his ladies sat up through long, long nights in the Bar, laughing with Captain Doubloon and drinking lots of punch, and sometimes Mr. Eleutherios played a sort of a guitar. By day they all lay out on the verandah in deck chairs in the shade, and complained that the sea was too loud.

And while they were all enjoying themselves, Emma and Masterman would help Winston clean up their rooms. At first Masterman grumbled a lot, but he soon became very proud of the way he could put the clean sheets on so smoothly they looked like newly fallen snow, without one wrinkle or crease. He became quite fussy if he didn't think Emma was doing it right.

At last Emma let him make all the beds himself. Instead, she would make sure there was fresh soap and clean towels in all the bathrooms, while Winston scrubbed the bathtubs. Mr. Eleutherios and his ladies always left their bathtubs a mess, full of squashed grapes.

There were no vacuum cleaners in the Grand Wenlocke, but Masterman found an old-fashioned carpet-sweeper. He took off the push-handle and invented a way to rig the sweeper up to a little harness. He put the harness on Shorty, who ran happily up and down the corridors pulling the sweeper to and fro.

When each room was tidy, Emma and Masterman would pick up big armfuls of sheets and towels and take them down to the Electrical Laundry. This was a vaulted hall under the hotel, opening off the Kitchens. All down one side of the room were giant tubs of hot water that filled from copper boilers, and the mechanism of the Difference Engine powered big paddles that sloshed round and round in the tubs.

Captain Doubloon worked down there in the mornings. He liked throwing the laundry in and adding soap flakes, but he didn't so much like hauling out the wet laundry afterward and putting it through the wringer, or trudging along between miles of clotheslines with his arms full of wet towels and his mouth full of clothespins, while his parrot made sarcastic remarks. Still, he was too proud to admit that sailors weren't better than anybody else at keeping things clean, so he did a good job and didn't curse where anybody but the parrot could hear him.

When any of the guests decided to go to the Dining Room, Masterman would serve as the maître d', in his long tailcoat, and show them to their places. Emma would give them their menus, which Mrs. Beet wrote out in ink every day, and then take their orders when they had decided what they wanted to eat. Winston would run down to the Kitchens with their orders, and when Mrs. Beet had loaded their plates, he would hurry back up with a big silver cart full of trays of food.

The Freets never ordered anything but dessert, like Cherries Jubilee or Baked Alaska. The People of the Sands had coffee with every meal, and put so much cream and sugar in it that the coffee was as thick as syrup. The beautiful people ate only lettuce and drank only water. Mr. Eleutherios and his lady friends had wine with every meal, even breakfast, and generally ordered roast lamb with rosemary and garlic.

Captain Doubloon ate down in the Kitchens, sharing a cozy table with Mrs. Beet and Shorty, but Emma and Masterman had their own table in the Dining Room. When all the guests had been waited on, Winston would wait on the two children. Emma felt very grand ordering veal cutlets or breaded sole or filet mignon, and sipping from her fine-cut crystal water glass.

19

ORPHANS

ONE MORNING, AS she was brushing her hair, Emma noticed that she felt light-hearted. As she thought about it, she realized that she had been light-hearted for quite a while now. It gave her a little shock to understand that it had been a long time since she had thought about the storm, or the people and things she had lost in the storm.

She had been so busy having adventures and making new friends that she hadn't had time to be sad. It made her feel guilty now. She was a little glum as she went down to breakfast, and a little silent as she sat across the table from Masterman.

"What's the matter with *you* today?" Masterman said at last.

Emma picked up her spoon and stirred her oatmeal around before answering. "Don't you ever feel bad about being an orphan?"

"I used to," said Masterman. "I felt bad all the time."

"What happened to your family?" asked Emma. "If you don't mind me asking."

"That's all right," said Masterman. "My father was The Astonishing Wenlocke. He was the greatest magician who ever lived, because his tricks weren't just illusions. He could work *real* magic."

"Is there real magic?"

"Of course there is. Look around," said Masterman, waving his spoon at the other people in the Dining Room. "Who do you think all these people are? They're magic. And Winston's a ghost! If you weren't very good at noticing things, you might not even see them, but we Wenlockes have always been able to see them."

"I can see them too," said Emma.

"Well, I suppose you're intelligent," said Masterman, a little grudgingly. "Or maybe it's because you're a kid. My father always told me that everyone starts out being able to see magic, but because it's scary, most people pretend it isn't there. By the time they grow up, they really can't see magical things anymore. That was the problem with my father's magic act." He sighed and looked down at the table.

"Why?"

"His magic tricks were real, and no one could figure out how they worked. People got angry that they couldn't figure out the tricks, especially the people who wrote stage reviews for newspapers. So they wrote bad reviews of his shows, and then no one would come to the shows after the second or third night. So we had to move around a lot. The Astonishing Wenlocke played in all the great cities of the world. We stayed in the very best hotels."

"Was it just you and your father?"

"No. My mother was in the act. 'The Astonishing Wenlocke and Melusine, his Lovely Assistant!' She had a beautiful costume with spangles and wore a tiara with feathers. And if the accident hadn't happened — " Masterman scowled, and jabbed his spoon into his grapefruit half so hard a squirt of grapefruit juice shot across the table. "I was going to be in the act too, as soon as I turned five. My mother would have made me a costume and everything."

"I'm sorry," said Emma.

"But one night they put me to bed in our room in the hotel, just as they always did," said Masterman. "And they kissed me goodnight and went off to the theater, just as they always did. When I woke up in the morning, I thought they'd be there, just as they always used to be, having breakfast. But that morning, they weren't.

"I waited and waited, and when they didn't come back I called Room Service and ordered my own breakfast. I had pancakes with four different kinds of syrup, and coffee with extra sugar, and ice cream. I ate breakfast and then I bounced on the beds, and then I bounced on the couch, and then I bounced on the armchairs.

"But my parents still hadn't come home by lunchtime. So I called Room Service and ordered lunch. I had chocolate cheesecake and orange soda and more coffee with extra sugar and ice cream. Then I bounced on the beds some more. Then I moved the furniture around and made a fort. Then I played with my father's stage makeup and drew a beard and mustache on myself.

"Dinnertime came, and I was just about to call Room Service when the door opened and the police came in. They told me there had been a mysterious accident. Both my parents had disappeared."

"What happened?" asked Emma.

"Well, there was a trick called the Vanishing Cabinet," said Masterman. "My mother would step into it and close the door. Then my father would open the door and she'd be gone. But then he'd close the door, spin the cabinet around, and open the door again, and she'd step out smiling and waving at the audience.

"But on that night she hadn't come back, no matter how many times my father spun the cabinet, and the audience began to boo and stamp their feet. So my father climbed inside the cabinet too and closed the door. I guess he was going to look for her. The audience waited and waited, but nothing happened, and at last the theater manager came out and opened the cabinet. No one was inside."

"Didn't anyone ever find them?" Emma asked.

Masterman shook his head, pressing his lips tight together.

He swallowed hard.

"So then I had to live in an orphanage for a few days until this rotten little man came and told me he was the Wenlocke family lawyer. He said I was going to be his ward now. I was supposed to call him Uncle Roderick."

"Did you?"

"No," said Masterman. "I called him Rotten Stinky Little Baldy."

"No wonder he didn't like you!"

"Well, I found out he had the Vanishing Cabinet burned," said Masterman. "Along with all my father's other magic stuff, because he said magic was wicked and dangerous. Because of that, my parents could never come back through the cabinet, even if they were still alive.

"And he thought I knew where the Wenlocke family treasure was. I told him there wasn't a treasure anymore, because of Great-Grandfather Masterman losing it when this place sank under the sand. But Uncle Roderick wouldn't believe me. He said he'd send me to Pavor Noctis Academy unless I told him the truth.

"And when he did send me there, it was horrible. The other boys got birthday presents and holiday presents from their parents, but all I ever got were cards from Uncle Roderick, and they always said the same thing: 'Dear Masterman, sorry I can't afford to send you any presents, but if I knew where the Wenlocke treasure was, you'd have a pony and a puppy of your very own. Too bad! How do you like the hard beds and bread and water meals at Pavor Noctis? If you want to leave, all you have to do is *tell me where the treasure is!*'"

"That's awful," said Emma. "That's just as bad as what happened to me. What did you do, when you felt scared and all alone?"

"I thought about my parents," said Masterman. "I knew that they wouldn't have let Uncle Roderick treat me the way he did. They would have wanted me to be all right. So I decided I *would* be all right, whatever Uncle Roderick tried to do. I would be brave and escape as soon as I could, and grow up somewhere, and then I'd become a magician.

"So I flew away! And here I am now, right where every Wenlocke has longed to be for a hundred years. So awful things happen sometimes, but good things can happen too. The trick is to be as brave as you can through the terrible parts so you can get to the wonderful ones, because they *will* come along someday," said Masterman.

"That's true," said Emma, looking around at the Grand Wenlocke.

"And when they come, you have to remember how to be happy again," Masterman added. "That's very important."

"But you can't ever forget the people you lose, can you?" said Emma.

"Of course not," said Masterman. He picked up his water glass and held it up. "Here's to making them proud of us!"

Emma held up her water glass too and they clinked glasses and drank. She felt better. She decided that Masterman was wise as well as brave, even if he was a brat most of the time.

20

THE PLAN

ONE DAY AS Emma and Masterman were bringing their seventeenth load of pillowcases down to the Electrical Laundry Room, they heard a lot of very bad language coming from behind a long row of drying top sheets.

"Ahem," said Emma.

The bad language stopped. Captain Doubloon glared out with his one eye from between two bath towels. "Oh, not more bloody laundry," he said.

"I'm afraid so," said Emma.

"And we have the whole third floor to make up, so I hope you've finished ironing the bottom sheets," said Masterman.

"No, I ain't, because I've had to wash all the tablecloths and napkins. Them blasted guests is got grape juice spilled all over 'em," said Captain Doubloon.

"Awk! Yo ho ho and a bottle of rum!" said the parrot.

"Shut up, you darned bird! Look here, kiddies, we needs more folk working here," said Captain Doubloon. "Chambermaids and laundresses and whatnot. This ain't no work for a sailor!"

"But where could we find any help?" said Masterman. "We're a long way from *ordinary* places. We can't exactly put a want ad in the paper."

"Winston could telegraph again," said Emma.

"So he could, but then, you might find maids turning up what's got fairy wings, or snakes for hair, or some such," said Captain Doubloon. "And I don't reckon magical folk make dependable housecleaners, somehow."

"You know, if you towed the hotel away to that tropical island you told us about, I'll bet we could advertise for more help there," said Emma.

Captain Doubloon's one eye shone like a lighthouse beam.

"So we could," he said. "And it might be a good idea to do it afore the next Storm of the Equinox too, so's we don't have the whole place going to Davy Jones's Locker again. And then, once we was settled, I could ask Mrs. Beet for her hand in marriage!"

"Marriage?" Masterman began to giggle. "You and Mrs. Beet?"

"You can keep yer snickers to yerself, you little whey-faced whelp," said Captain Doubloon. "Mrs. Beet's a fine woman, and good cooking lasts a sight longer than good looks, let me tell you. Besides, she likes me as much as I likes her."

"Two eyes, one heart?" said Masterman, grinning.

"Aye," sighed Captain Doubloon. "It's like we was made for each other. *Neddy dear,* she calls me."

Masterman would have started laughing again, but Emma stepped firmly on his foot and said, "That's lovely, and I'm very happy for you. Will it take very long to get the hotel ready to travel?"

"Not more'n a few days, I reckon," said Captain Doubloon.

"We'd better go tell Winston, then," said Masterman.

But when they told Winston, he looked worried.

"It's certainly a good idea to move the Grand Wenlocke to a safer place," he said. "We do need a bigger staff, and I'd love to hire a band so we could have dances in the ballroom. But how are we going to move the hotel when it's got guests staying here? Some of them have paid for months and months ahead."

"I know what we'll do," said Emma. She told her plan to Winston and Masterman, who agreed that it was a good one. So Emma and Masterman went out to the verandah where Mr. Eleutherios and his lady friends liked to relax.

"Excuse me," said Emma.

"Yiasou!" said Mr. Eleutherios cheerily.

"Excuse me, everyone! The staff and management of the Grand Wenlocke would like to make an announcement. In just a few days, you will all receive a fabulous complimentary sea cruise to a beautiful tropical paradise. You won't even have to leave your rooms!"

Mr. Eleutherios and the ladies just stared at her. Masterman cleared his throat and began to translate what Emma had said into Greek. Emma could tell when he had finished, because Mr. Eleutherios shouted *"Opa!"* and began to play a dance tune on his guitar, and all his ladies smiled broadly and shouted *"Opa!"* too.

"That went pretty well," said Emma, picking grapes out of her hair as they left.

"I hope the others take it as nicely," said Masterman, untwining a twig of grapevine from his lapel.

They went next to the Theater where the beautiful people were, but they had to turn off the projector and turn on the lights before the beautiful people would notice them. Emma repeated her announcement and Masterman translated for her once again. It sounded a lot like Greek too, except that every sentence seemed to begin and end with the word *dahhhhhhlings.* When he had finished, the beautiful people all looked blank and then began shouting questions. Emma could tell that Masterman was answering as best he could, but he looked flustered and angry by the time they were able to leave the theater.

"What did they want to know?" asked Emma.

"All sorts of things," said Masterman. "Like would they still be able to use their hair dryers, and could we positively guarantee no newpaper photographers would bother them, and could we please hire more servants to come work at the hotel. Especially a plastic surgeon."

"Well, maybe we can find one on the tropical island," said Emma.

Next they went to the Natatorium, and Emma made her announcement to the People of the Sand. They all swam to the edges of the pool as she spoke, to give her their full attention. Even the camels seemed to be listening intently. When Masterman translated for her, in a language that sounded like the hissing of wind across the Dunes and gusts thundering up into the sky, they turned to one another and conferred among themselves. At last one of them asked a question. Masterman's reply was short, and seemed to satisfy them, for they went back to swimming laps.

"They wanted to know if there would be sandy beaches where we're going," Masterman explained to Emma as they left the Natatorium. "I told them of course there would be. All tropical islands have sandy beaches, don't they?"

"Some only have rocks," said Emma. Masterman waved his hand dismissively.

"We'll just pick one with sand," he said.

The last place they went was the Conservatory, where the Freets were basking in the warmth. Emma didn't bother to make the announcement this time, but let Masterman make it, in the strange twittering language spoken by the Freets. Mr. Freet responded with a question, and Masterman replied. The Freets nodded, and reclined once more on their lounge chairs.

"They just wanted to know if there would be flowers there," Masterman told Emma.

"If there aren't any, we'll plant some," said Emma.

Captain Doubloon got very busy, bringing oil drums and steel cables from his boat. He spent the next few days going round and round the outside of the verandah, lashing the drums into place so that they would keep the hotel afloat at sea. Winston got all the spare clothesline from the Laundry, and carefully put a few safety loops about the bigger pieces of furniture, so that they wouldn't fall over if the hotel encountered rough seas on its journey.

But he wouldn't go outside to help Captain Doubloon carry oil drums from the ship. "Why in blazes not?" demanded Captain Doubloon. "It ain't like anything could hurt you, what with you being dead and all."

"I don't know why," said Winston, wringing his hands. "I just have this sort of feeling that I'm not supposed to leave the Grand Wenlocke. I've tried going out on the verandah, and I felt so insubstantial it gave me quite a nasty turn. I'll work extra hard looking after the guests, if someone else can go out for me. *Out there* — "He shuddered. "That's just sand and dreams, shadows and fog. I might blow away like mist, *out there.*"

"That's all right," said Masterman. "I'll go out and help you, Captain."

Emma looked at him in astonishment. Masterman had certainly improved from the haughty little creature he had been when he first came to the Grand Wenlocke.

"Well, thank 'ee, lad, but a shrimp like you ain't going to be much use," grumbled Captain Doubloon.

"I'll go too," said Emma. "If we both try, we can lift a barrel between us."

"We'll see," said Captain Doubloon, but he didn't sound as though he believed they could do any good.

All the same, when Emma and Masterman walked out through the Dunes to the beach, they found it easy work. The oil drums, being empty, weren't very heavy — they were just awkward. Emma found an old fishing net that had been lost from some trawler. She and Masterman worked out a way to fill it with several barrels at a time and drag it behind them, with Shorty gripping a piece of the net in his jaws too and running beside them. They dragged the barrels all the way to where the captain was digging under the hotel. He took the barrels and chained them in place.

The children made a lot of trips back and forth, managing to get the rest of the oil drums up from the beach in a few days. Though they were very, very tired when night came, Mrs. Beet always fixed a nice hot supper for them. And Winston, true to his word, worked twice as hard and saw to all the laundry and the cleaning for the guests.

At last everything was ready. Just after sunrise, on a morning when the wind was blowing hard from inshore, Captain Doubloon went out to his boat with Emma while Masterman and Mrs. Beet went once around the outside of the Grand Wenlocke to make certain that everything was fastened tight. Winston shepherded the hotel guests into the Bar, where they eagerly awaited the sea voyage. Then Masterman went up to Emma's turret room with a pistol that Captain Doubloon had given him, and waited.

Emma climbed out of the rowboat and up the rusty ladder to the deck of Captain Doubloon's ship. There was certainly a lot of rust, but she knew it wouldn't be polite to say so. "What's the name of this ship?" she asked instead.

"She's the *By-the-Wind-Sailor*," said Captain Doubloon, puffing and panting as he came aboard. "Don't look like much, do she? But she's got a powerful strong engine. She used to work as a tugboat, hauling them big cruise liners in and out of harbors. When one of 'em would get stuck on a sandbar, why, they'd radio for the *By-the-Wind-Sailor*, and she'd pull 'em free in less time than it takes to sing 'Fifteen Men on a Dead Man's Chest'! That's why I, er, saved up and bought her. If any boat could pull a hotel across the sea, *By-the-Wind-Sailor*'s the one to do it, by thunder!"

He handed Emma a spyglass. "You watch that little lubber up

in the turret, now, and tell me when he's ready to give the signal. I'll get the engines warmed up."

Emma opened the spyglass and looked back across the Dunes to the Grand Wenlocke. There was her turret room, with the seaward window wide open, and Masterman leaned out of it with the pistol cocked and held up in the air for safety, as though he were a miniature spy. He was watching the horizon keenly.

"He's ready, Captain," Emma shouted, over the roar of the *By-the-Wind-Sailor*'s engines.

"Right then!" Captain Doubloon shouted back. "See that there gun on the port bow? You get ready to fire it off when I gives the word!"

Fortunately Emma knew that the port side was the left side of the ship, because *port* and *left* both have four letters. She ran to the little signal cannon there and took hold of its firing cord. The engines roared louder and louder, and water foamed like white lace all around the ship's hull. A moment or two they rose and fell on the surge, and then Captain Doubloon shouted, "FIRE!"

Emma pulled sharply on the cord, and the cannon fired a shot that echoed across the rolling water. She grabbed up the telescope and peered through it just in time to see the puff of white smoke rising as Masterman fired his pistol, letting everyone in the hotel know it was time to brace themselves.

Captain Doubloon took the wheel of the *By-the-Wind-Sailor* and let her out, and she headed out to sea. Emma, watching over her stern, saw the cable chain rise dripping from the water as it pulled taut. It jerked, and jumped tight as a guitar-string, sending drops of water flying everywhere.

"The hotel is beginning to move!" cried Emma, watching through the spyglass as the Grand Wenlocke jolted forward a foot or so. Only a little further, and it began to slide across the sand. It moved so easily that Emma wondered if it hadn't been designed to travel all along. She could see a little of the foundation under the Difference Engine now, and it seemed to be smooth and curved, like the hull of a ship. Perhaps that had been why it had sunk under the sand in the first place.

But, just as everything seemed to be going well, Emma heard another pistol shot. She swung the spyglass up to look at the turret room. There was no sign of Masterman, though she could see Mifficent the doll. Was she waving her arms? Or was that Emma's imagination?

Emma searched with the spyglass and spotted Masterman. He had run down to the verandah, and Mrs. Beet was beside him. They were both waving their arms and shouting. Shorty ran around and around their feet, barking like mad. Emma couldn't hear them, but it looked like something was wrong.

"We have to stop, Captain!" she yelled.

21

THE GHOST

CAPTAIN DOUBLOON LOWERED the rowboat from the *By-the-Wind-Sailor* again, and he and Emma climbed down and rowed quickly ashore. Emma jumped out and splashed up the beach. She ran quickly ahead of the Captain to the verandah of the Grand Wenlocke. To her dismay, she saw that Mrs. Beet was crying. Shorty was whimpering and trying to jump into her arms.

"What's the matter?" Emma shouted.

"It's poor Winston!" said Mrs. Beet. "Everything was going so well, and the hotel had begun to move, when suddenly he gave a dreadful shriek and — and — "

"It was like something pulled him through the wall!" said Masterman.

"But where is he?" said Emma.

"We don't know!" said Mrs. Beet, holding a handkerchief to her eye. "We asked all the guests, but they haven't seen him."

"Then let's look for him!" said Emma, and she ran along the verandah calling for Winston, as Masterman ran with her.

They had run halfway around the building, hearing only their hard shoes pounding on the wooden planks and the soft wailing of the wind across the sand, when Emma noticed what appeared to be a wisp of fog. It was hovering right over the gigantic track the Grand Wenlocke had left in the sand. Emma stopped short, and Masterman collided with her.

"Watch what you're doing!" he said angrily. But she held up her hand.

"Listen!" Emma said. They listened, and they heard a faint sad noise, very much like the sighing of the wind, only with words they couldn't quite make out. It was coming from the foggy shape. "That's Winston!"

"Oh, no!" said Masterman. Emma scrambled over the rail of the verandah and dropped down on the sand to run to the shape.

It was Winston, all right. He was more transparent than he had been the first time she had met him, in the Dunes, and he didn't seem to know that she was there. He hung in the wind, twisting and turning as though he were in terrible pain, lamenting softly. His kind face was so sad that Emma wanted to cry.

But she didn't cry. She stamped her foot in the sand and turned to Masterman. "We've got to help him!"

Masterman was still on the verandah, staring at Winston in horror, and Emma realized he was frightened. "Do you know what's wrong with him?" she demanded.

"He's not supposed to leave the hotel," said Masterman. "But — I guess when we moved it, the hotel left *him.*"

"But why didn't he go with it? Why is he stuck here?" said Emma, but even as she asked, she began to have an idea what the answer might be. "Oh! When the hotel went under the sand, he was pitched out of it — and he was trying to find it when the storm caught him and he died — and so — "

"He was buried too," said Masterman, who had gone very pale. "And his body must be here someplace. He can't leave as long as his body is here."

Both the children were silent for a moment as the horrible truth sank in on them. All the while Winston's spirit had been happily working inside the Grand Wenlocke, his mortal remains had been lying somewhere underneath it, lost in the sand.

Emma turned and ran toward the front steps. "What are you going to do?" said Masterman, running along the verandah.

"*We* are going to get a couple of shovels and dig up Winston's body," said Emma.

"But he'll be a shriveled-up mummy, or even a skeleton!" said Masterman. "And it may take us days to find him!"

"I don't care!" said Emma. "We can't leave him here."

Emma told Mrs. Beet and Captain Doubloon, who had arrived from the beach at last, what they were going to do. Captain Doubloon obligingly pulled a couple of small shovels from inside his coat and handed them to the children.

"If I was you, I'd dig under the place where his ghost is crying," he said.

"Neddy, dearest, you can't let the children go by themselves!" said Mrs. Beet. "Go on, the three of you, and save Winston! I'll go see to the guests."

Emma grabbed Masterman by the hand and pulled him with her as she ran back behind the hotel. Shorty galloped after them, and Captain Doubloon followed at a distance, puffing and panting as he stumped along.

When they got back to where Winston's specter drifted, Emma called out, "Don't worry, Winston! We'll get you back in the hotel somehow!"

"I don't think he can hear you," said Masterman sourly.

"What are you being so crabby for?" said Emma, plunging her shovel into the sand.

"Corpses scare me, that's all," said Masterman. "Silly of me, but there it is."

"Well, life is full of scary things," said Emma, as she dug.

"That's true, but we Wenlockes see more of them than most people," said Masterman. "People think it must be wonderful to see fairies and unicorns and all that, but they don't know about the awful things that exist right beside them. It's why children learn to pretend magic isn't real. If you saw the things I used to see in my dreams at night, you'd never sleep again."

Emma thought about the dark cold rooms that had been Mr. Wenlocke's, and decided *she* would never be brave enough to spend the night in there.

"Does your great-grandfather haunt his old rooms?" she asked Masterman.

"No," Masterman replied. "He just put so much magical protection in there it cast shadows all over the place. It's supposed to seem scary, to outsiders. But I don't mind it, because I know what it is."

"Then you shouldn't mind this, either," Emma said. "This isn't just any old corpse. This is Winston we're trying to find, and he's our friend, and you'll never keep the hotel running without him. So let's dig!"

Shorty was already helping out, scrabbling away with his little forepaws as fast as he could. Masterman set to work too. Captain Doubloon arrived at last, gasping slightly, and watched their progress.

They dug and dug and dug, and found nothing but sand for the longest time, as the ghost moaned in midair above them. Dry sand kept sliding back downhill into the hole they were making. But then —

"Here's a shoe!" said Masterman.

"Where?" Emma bent down to see. Sticking out of the sand was an old black leather shoe. It was dull and had cracked and curled up with age, but looked as though it might once have been one of Winston's perfectly polished shoes.

"Is there a foot still in it?" asked Masterman, hiding his eyes.

"Er — I reckon I'd best take over now," said Captain Doubloon. "You come on out of there, lass. This ain't likely to be a pretty sight."

"No," said Emma, exploring with the edge of the shovel. "I can do this." She thought about Winston fetching her a clamshell of water when she had first arrived at the Dunes, and how he had helped her to survive the night of the sandstorm. She knew that whatever scary thing might be buried beneath her feet, she had a duty to find it for Winston. She dug carefully, freeing the shoe.

Masterman leaned down and grabbed up Shorty before the little dog could pounce on the shoe. Right next to the shoe was a second shoe, and underneath them…

"It's Winston's hat," she said, and had to bite her lip very hard to keep from crying. Cautiously she lifted it out, and saw that she had not made a mistake: it was Winston's white Bell Captain's hat, though it too was cracked and shriveled with age. But its gold badge still gleamed brightly, and so did the twenty brass buttons that were piled up inside it, along with a double handful of strange white dust.

Masterman stared at the dust with eyes like saucers.

"That's all that's left of him," he said. Emma realized that the relentless blowing sands had so scoured and polished poor Winston's bones that they had ground them down to powder, white as angel wings.

"It's *not* all that's left of him," said Emma, blinking back tears. "It's just all that's left of his old body. Come on!"

She picked up the shoes too and marched back to the Grand Wenlocke. The crying wraith was pulled after her, like a balloon on a string. Shorty jumped from Masterman's arms and ran along too. After a moment Masterman followed behind, dragging the two shovels. Captain Doubloon followed as fast as he could, but he still hadn't caught his breath yet, so he wheezed like an old accordion.

They went straight up the verandah steps and into the Lobby. The guests had come into the Lobby from the Bar and were standing around anxiously. Even the beautiful people, who usually took no notice of anyone but themselves, looked worried.

On the threshold Emma paused, wondering what to do next. She remembered that sometimes people keep the ashes of people they loved in fancy vases. There was a pair of tall, particularly elegant vases, all blue and white and gold, on either side of the front desk. As the guests in the Lobby watched, she went to the nearest one and dropped Winston's shoes in, and followed them with the hat full of dust.

WHOOSH! A pair of bright-gleaming stars appeared in mid-air, just about at eye level. Then a golden star appeared above it, and twenty lesser gold stars below, Winston's Bell Captain's badge and buttons, and then Winston stood again, quite real and solid.

"Hurrah!" he cried. "Heaven again! Thank you, Miss Emma! Thank you, Master Masterman!"

All the guests applauded, and Mr. Eleutherios played a celebratory tune on his guitar while his ladies danced. Mrs. Beet dropped a whole tray of canapés in her headlong rush to throw her arms around Winston and kiss him on the cheek. Shorty leaped gratefully onto the tray and munched up all the little watercress sandwiches and petits fours. Winston kissed Mrs. Beet back, and then he saluted.

"Ladies and Gentlemen!" Winston shouted. "We regret the slight delay, but are dee-lighted to inform you that the Grand Wenlocke will now commence its ocean cruise!"

So they started up the *By-the-Wind-Sailor* again, and the Grand Wenlocke inched ahead over the Dunes, down at last to the flat wet beach. Crabs scuttled in all directions from its colossal progress across the sand. Seagulls screamed in alarm as the whole vast building slid on, a few feet at a time. A wave broke against the frontmost barrels, and then another. The *By-the-Wind-Sailor* surged ahead, gaining speed. Suddenly the Grand Wenlocke lurched forward and bobbed a moment in the deeper water, before moving majestically out to sea.

22

At Sea

The Grand Wenlocke fared quite well on the open sea, cruising along so smoothly there were scarcely any ripples in the soup that Mrs. Beet served at luncheon. But there was no soup for Masterman; for, the moment they were afloat, Masterman had turned an unpleasant shade of green and begun to sweat.

"What's wrong with you?" Emma asked him.

"What do you think is wrong with me?" Masterman groaned.

"Are you seasick?"

"No!" But it was plain that was exactly what was wrong. He turned away from her, but there in front of him were the big lobby windows, with the blue sea surging away outside, up and down, and cheerful whitecaps breaking on the veranda railings and splashing foam on the steps.

"Oh — " Masterman looked around, desperation in his eyes. Emma looked around too. While Victorian hotels were beautiful and grand, it is a sad fact that their bathrooms were usually located inconveniently far away, if indeed they were indoors at all. The Grand Wenlocke, being the very finest of its kind, had all its bathrooms indoors; but not within running distance of the Lobby, unfortunately.

"Oh — " Masterman began to stagger back and forth in a hopeless kind of way.

"Go out on the verandah and hang over the rail!" said Emma, trying to grab his arm. He just shook his head, pressing his lips tight together. At last he turned and ran down the stairs to the Kitchen, narrowly missing Winston who was coming up with a tray of light snacks for the gentlemen guests in the Bar. The snacks were anchovies and little sardines on toast, and pickled eggs, and sliced onions and caviar in pastry puffs. Masterman made a horrified sound as he dove past Winston, clapping his hands to his mouth.

"What's the matter?" Winston called out, as Emma raced after Masterman.

"Seasick!" Emma shouted, and then added, "Him, not me!"

Masterman made it all the way to the bottom of the stairs before doubling up. Mrs. Beet, who was just sliding a pan of biscuits into the oven, turned in astonishment as he opened his mouth —

And out fell a green dragonfly. And another. And then a whole string of others, in blue and orange. They all looked as though they had just hatched, with their wings damp and crumpled. As Emma and Mrs. Beet stared, they one by one unfolded their wings and fluttered them. One or two lifted off and began to circle the room. Shorty, who had been dozing in his basket bed, woke up and noticed them. He leaped out and began to run in circles, barking and now and then making little jumps in the air at the dragonflies.

"What have you been eating?" said Emma. Masterman, clutching the stair rail, just gasped for breath and shook his head.

"Oh, dear," said Mrs. Beet. "Seasick, is he?"

"He's throwing up bugs!" said Emma. This made Masterman groan again, and then there were three red dragonflies and a luna moth opening their wings on the floor.

"What I heard was, Mr. Wenlocke's brother used to do the same," said Mrs. Beet, wiping her hands on her apron. "Couldn't cross water to save his life. Had to travel by train or balloon anywhere he went, or he'd be coughing up orchids. It's just one of those Wenlocke things. You sit down and put your head on your knees, dear. Now, what was it that was supposed to help? Ginger ale with some sort of flower petals steeped in it, I recollect. Was it roses? Or tulips?"

"I don't want anything," said Masterman tearfully, and a

monarch butterfly dropped out on his shoes. "No — no, I want to die."

"Don't be silly," said Emma, waving away the dragonflies, which were all flying about now. She was about to add that it was only seasickness, but decided not to, because Masterman was really miserable. Besides, Wenlocke seasickness didn't seem to be like seasickness for anyone else.

In the end Winston carried him upstairs and set him on a chaise lounge in the Lobby, where he was draped with a shawl and lay limp, with his eyes tight closed. His face was still a delicate pea-green, and every so often he'd hiccup, upon which another dragonfly or perhaps a flight of moths would pop out. Soon there were several brightly colored tropical butterflies flitting up near the ceiling, where they were greatly admired by the hotel guests.

For three days, as they steamed along, he could take nothing but a few orange blossoms simmered in ginger sauce. Emma was a little annoyed that he was unable to do any of his duties, because she already had the extra work of passing Captain Doubloon's meals over in the basket they had rigged on a clothesline and pulley. But, since it wasn't Masterman's fault he was sick, and since complaining wouldn't help in any case, she just did what she had to do.

On the morning of the fourth day, however, Masterman had much more than seasickness to worry about.

23

The Disparagement

Emma had just finished clearing away the guests' breakfast plates with Winston when she became aware of a noise echoing over the sea. She ran to the dining room window and looked out. Far off to starboard was a yacht, cutting over the white waves at great speed. It looked as though it might be trying to intercept the *By-the-Wind-Sailor*.

As it drew nearer, the noise came echoing out again, much louder now. Someone on the deck of the yacht was shouting into a bullhorn. *"Stop! Stop in the name of the law! Heave to!"*

But the *By-the-Wind-Sailor* just kept steaming ahead. Emma shaded her eyes and stared very hard at the yacht as it sailed closer. It looked like somebody's luxury craft.

"What the heck is that?" said Winston, coming to the window

to look over her shoulder.

"I think it's trouble," said Emma.

"Stop! Stop, thieves!" The voice cried over the bullhorn.

"What do they mean, *thieves?*" said Winston angrily. "We haven't stolen anything."

"And they aren't the police," said Emma. "That's not a police boat, and it hasn't got any Coast Guard signs on it, either. I hope Captain Doubloon doesn't stop for them."

"I don't think he will, somehow," said Winston.

In fact, the *By-the-Wind-Sailor* seemed to speed up, and the Grand Wenlocke bounded over the sea in a way that would make anyone a little queasy. But the yacht kept on coming. Soon it was close enough to see clearly the man standing in the bow, calling through the bullhorn. He was a small man, though his head was rather large and perfectly bald. He clearly thought of himself as a dashing fellow, for he wore a yachtsman's fancy blazer and a too-small yachting cap perched on his domed head.

"He doesn't look so tough," said Emma.

"No, but *they* do," said Winston, pointing. All along the rail stood some men in black uniforms. "You know, I think I'll just invite the guests down to the Theater. I'll come back as soon as I've put on one of those cinematograph reels — they're as good as a magician doing tricks to hold people's attention. That way, the guests won't notice if there's any unpleasantness."

"What unpleasantness?" said a faint voice from the chaise lounge. Masterman sat up unsteadily. "What's going on?"

He staggered in from the Lobby and joined Emma at the window, as Winston ran to talk to the guests. Emma pointed out the yacht. Masterman peered at it, and then went (though Emma would not have thought it possible) an even paler shade of chalky pistachio.

"Oh, no! That's Uncle Roderick!" he cried.

"You mean the man who sent you to the military school?"

"Yes! And he hates me!"

"He must have found out about the Grand Wenlocke reappearing," said Emma, watching as the yacht got closer, and wishing she had Captain Doubloon's cutlass.

"Where's the rest of the breakfast dishes?" demanded Mrs. Beet, huffing and puffing from her climb up the stairs. Shorty came running after her, yapping excitedly. "Nothing's come down in the dumbwaiter for five minutes and — oh, blimey, what's that?"

"It's Masterman's guardian," said Emma.

"Really?" Mrs. Beet scowled. "I suppose he'll want to take the child back to that school now. However did he find us?"

"He must have been hunting for me," said Masterman. "He knew I'd go to the Dunes!"

"But how'd he know we were back in business?"

"There are these things nowadays, called satellites," said

Emma. "They're like giant spyglasses in the sky. Maybe he had a way to look at satellite pictures."

"How inconvenient," said Mrs. Beet.

"Or maybe he had spies in his pay," said Masterman dramatically. "If the hotel guests found us, other people might have. Look at him! Doesn't he look like a middle-aged goblin?"

By this time the yacht had veered very close indeed, and the voice screeching from its bullhorn was clear and unmistakable: *"Stop! Stop in the name of the Wenlocke Family Trust! That hotel is stolen property!"*

"Ha!" said Mrs. Beet. She threw open the window and shouted, "You're wrong, there! Who should own this hotel but a Wenlocke, I'd like to know? And here he is!" She grabbed Masterman by the scruff of his jacket and the seat of his pants, and held him up in the window. Shorty jumped up and down, barking wildly, trying to see out the window.

Masterman was terrified. "No!" he squeaked. "You don't understand! He's evil!"

Emma had a terrible feeling he was right. The man in yachting clothes spotted Masterman, and the expression on his face was not at all what it should have been if he had been worried over Masterman and eager to see him safe.

Emma knew that grown people can sometimes be surprisingly blind to evil things, and so she grabbed Mrs. Beet's arm. "We're in danger! Let's get away from the window!"

"Eh? But that's his guardian, child. He wouldn't harm our Masterman," said Mrs. Beet.

The man in the yachting clothes rubbed his hands together and shrieked in glee. *"Haha! There you are, Masterman! You've been a very naughty boy!"* He turned and said something to one of the others on deck, who passed the message to the man at the wheel.

The yacht swung about and revealed her stern, on which was the name *DISPARAGEMENT* in gold letters. Emma did not spend much time spelling this out, however, for she was busy watching as a hatch slid back from the stern and a platform rose slowly up to the deck from below.

"Get away from the window!" shouted Winston, running up behind them. "That's a gun deck!" He tackled Mrs. Beet in a flying leap and they went down with Masterman, just as there was a flash of light from the direction of the yacht.

Emma dropped flat too, and heard the *boom* and the whistle overhead as a cannonball shot in through the open window. It smashed into a panel at the rear of the Dining Room.

"Dear me, Masterman, did they miss? What a shame. Now you'll have to go back to your classmates!" cried Uncle Roderick. "Minions, reload!"

"See? I told you he wanted to kill me!" said Masterman. Shorty crouched beside him, growling.

"Oh, dear, the watered-silk wallpaper — " said Mrs. Beet distractedly.

"They've damaged the hotel!" said Winston, looking angrier than Emma had ever seen him. *"They've damaged the hotel!"*

"And tried to kill me, too," said Masterman.

"You'll stand to attention in the rain, Masterman! You'll peel hundreds and thousands of potatoes! You'll scrub thousands and millions of pots! You'll march millions and billions of miles!" shouted Uncle Roderick. "Hahahaaaa!"

"Don't listen to him," Emma told Masterman. "He's just trying to get you to yell back, so he can see where you are."

"I won't stand for this!" Winston scrambled to his feet, and Emma almost shouted to him to get down, before she remembered he was already dead. "No sir, I won't! Where's that emergency lever!"

He strode into the Lobby. *Crash,* another cannonball shattered a window! *Thwap,* it buried itself in the oak paneling, but Winston ignored it as he stepped behind the desk.

Emma followed him as far as the doorway, keeping almost flat to the floor and crawling behind furniture whenever she could. Winston opened the glass case and yanked hard on the lever there. Emma heard a deep grinding sound from somewhere down under the floorboards. Suddenly, a section of the marble floor slid back, and something of gleaming gray steel rose up and forward from below. As it moved into place, the Lobby doors opened automatically.

"We have our own cannon?" Emma asked.

"We certainly do," replied Winston. "My Mr. Wenlocke, he was no fool."

"Thank you, Great-Grandfather!" said Masterman from his hiding place in the dining room.

"Oh, Masterman! It was wicked of you to run off like that, and leave your poor dear guardian wondering where you were! Everyone at good old Pavor Noctis has given you up for dead, you know! Why, if something awful were to happen to you right now, no one would ever hear about it!" yelled Uncle Roderick from his yacht.

"Oh, shut up!" said Masterman, but very quietly. He grabbed Shorty, who was growling and snapping as though he'd like to jump out the window and attack Uncle Roderick himself.

On the platform beside the cannon, behind a blast shield of plate steel, was a neat pyramid of stacked shot canisters. Emma scrambled to it, keeping well behind a sofa until she was there. Winston was already opening the loading chamber of the gun when Emma handed him a canister. He slid it into the breech and rammed it shut.

"May I fire it?" asked Emma. Like most well-brought-up children, she had always wanted to shoot off a real cannon.

"Don't be silly, dear, that's nothing a little girl should be doing," said Mrs. Beet, who had followed her. "You might kill someone, after all. Let *me* fire it."

"Just *somebody* fire it!" begged Masterman, who had crawled behind one of the marble columns, holding Shorty tightly in his arms.

"What do you mean, turn and run?" On his yacht, Uncle Roderick had turned to berate a minion. "Look at that hotel! It'll make us millions! Watch for the boy! The minute he sticks his head up, fire! MASTERMAN, THIS IS YOUR LAST CHANCE TO COME OUT!"

The yacht swooped in close, for her crew hoped to get a broadside in, and it threw a drenching bow wave up that splashed through the broken windows.

"Why, those — that'll ruin the paneling!" said Winston. As he stood straight up in his indignation, the gunner on the yacht had a clear shot at him, and fired. Close as they were, the shot went right through the Lobby, and through Winston too. Emma and Mrs. Beet had thrown themselves flat, so they didn't see the moment of impact, though they heard the smash as the ball hit the front desk.

Emma looked up cautiously through all the smoke, not knowing what to expect. She didn't think anything very terrible had happened, since Winston was already dead, but she saw Masterman looking up in horror. Shorty whimpered. She rolled over and saw a great gray plume of smoke coiling up from where Winston had been standing. She heard a noise like a man roaring in anger.

As she watched, the smoke was joined by a thread of ashes and whirling sand, seeping from the urn in the Lobby. It thickened and flowed out the broken window, seeming to stretch out two dark arms. There were no gold buttons, no stars: only a terrible shadow with the suggestion of bones. She just glimpsed it becoming something very scary indeed as it extended out on the verandah. The laughter of the men on the yacht broke off. They began to yell in terror instead as the dark thing flowed over the water toward them.

"Now, child!" Mrs. Beet scrambled up and grabbed the lanyard that fired the cannon. "Get me another canister!"

She yanked the lanyard and the cannon fired. The canister exploded, peppering the yacht with small shot. One ball plucked Uncle Roderick's bullhorn right out of his hand, and the others whizzed through the yacht's sails, leaving neat round holes.

"Stop! What are you doing?" wailed Uncle Roderick. "Give them another broadside — Oh! What are you? *Keep away from me!*"

Emma loaded the cannon again. This time Mrs. Beet aimed it, because the yacht was now speeding away on another tack. Emma got to fire the cannon at last, but it didn't do much harm, because the yacht was flying out of range as fast as her tattered sails would take her. The shot kicked up the white water in her wake in a satisfying way. There was a double blast on the whistle from the *By-the-Wind-Sailor*, as Captain Doubloon signaled triumph.

"You cowards!" Masterman shouted gleefully after the yacht. He crawled from behind the column and stood up. "Nice shooting, ladies!"

The cloudy darkness that had been out on the verandah now seemed to spill back in through the broken windows, like the vapor from dry ice. It trickled along the floor, growing brighter and more solid as it came together, and mounded up in a sort of pillar shape beside the big vase in the Lobby. For a moment Emma glimpsed the grisly grim specter that had frightened Uncle Roderick away, before Winston resumed his old friendly appearance.

"I must apologize," he said. "I hope I didn't scare you. It's not an awfully nice shape to take, but, by gosh, I was so darned mad! *Look* at the mess they've made!"

"Look at them go!" said Masterman, running to the window. The yacht was fast disappearing over the horizon. "So much for you, Uncle Roderick!"

24

THE ISLAND

THERE WAS NO further pursuit by wicked Uncle Roderick. No bully is a match for a dreadful ghost, nor for two determined ladies with a cannon.

Emma and Masterman swept up the broken glass and splinters, while Winston went into the storerooms to see what might be there to repair things. He found plenty of glass, putty, and spare paneling on hand.

The only thing of which there wasn't any extra was the watered-silk wallpaper, but after digging the cannonball out and sanding the edges of the hole smooth, they hung a painting of a peaceful country brook over it. You would hardly have known there had been any disturbance at all — at least, not once the cannon was retracted back under the Lobby floor.

They saw many interesting things during the rest of the voyage, such as leaping dolphins and spouting whales, and albatrosses with wings big as airplanes. The guests, who had noticed the noise of the sea battle but assumed it was sound effects for the cinematograph, played shuffleboard on the verandah when the weather was fine.

At last they came in sight of a beautiful green mountain rising from the sea, with waterfalls and palm groves. There were pink and green parrots chattering in the groves, pulling flowers from the hibiscus bushes. There were green meadows and clear pools of water. But there was no hotel whatsoever for anyone who might land there. Captain Doubloon cut the engines on the *By-the-Wind-Sailor* and lay her to, and came out on deck to call across to the hotel.

"Here it is! If this wasn't a desert island, there'd be no end of cruise ships stopping here. We give folks some nice civilized amenities and they'll be lining up to go ashore!"

"This looks like a nice place," said Emma to Winston, who had come with her to the verandah. The guests, who had been having breakfast in the Dining Room, all rushed to the windows and exclaimed in admiration. Mrs. Beet hurried up from the Kitchens. Even Masterman struggled to his feet and came staggering out.

"Oh, it's *land!*" he said fervently. "Let's stop here!"

"What do you think?" Emma asked Winston. "Would we be able to run the hotel from here?"

"Well, sure," Winston said. "Look at all that fine scenery, and fresh water!"

"Oh, my, look at all those coconuts," said Mrs. Beet. "I can bake fresh coconut custard pies."

"Please don't talk about food," said Masterman, turning green again. "Drop anchor here, Captain!"

So Captain Doubloon dropped anchor in the blue bay. He came over to the hotel in his rowboat, and for a while went back and forth, ferrying people ashore.

The beautiful people set up beach chairs on the sand, put on sunglasses, and immediately lay down and basked in the sun. The Freets went at once to the hibiscus bushes and wandered among them, exclaiming happily in their strange speech. The People of the Sands led their camels off to graze under the palm trees.

Mr. Eleutherios and his lady friends gathered coconuts and pineapples, and very quickly invented a new kind of fruit punch. They found a shady place under the trees and threw a party. Mr. Eleutherios played surfing songs on his guitar.

"Well, it looks like the guests are having a lovely time," said Emma. She squinted up at the Grand Wenlocke, where it bobbed quietly offshore, just beyond the breakers. Winston stood at the window, looking out wistfully. She waved to him. "The only problem we have now is how to get the hotel ashore."

"That's no problem at all," said Masterman, who sprawled in the warm sand with Shorty curled up at his feet. "See those big palm trunks up there? We just run the cable around them and use some pulleys to winch the hotel onto the land."

"How d'you reckon we'll manage?" said Captain Doubloon. "The guests ain't going to take kindly to being asked to haul on the cables, and we can't do it alone."

"Don't be silly!" said Masterman, in such a superior voice Captain Doubloon scowled at him. "I can do it myself, once we get everything arranged according to plan."

"A shrimp like you?" Captain Doubloon roared with laughter. "Not likely! I'll bet you half me treasure you can't do it."

Masterman leaped to his feet, causing Shorty to jump up in excitement. *Uh-oh,* thought Emma, seeing the gleam in Masterman's eyes.

"The bet's on!" said Masterman. "You have obviously never heard of Archimedes."

"Who?" said Captain Doubloon.

"There's an encyclopedia in the library. Look him up sometime," said Masterman, as he ran for the boat. "Come on, Emma!"

Captain Doubloon had to row them out and help them unhook the cable drum from the *By-the-Wind-Sailor,* and he helped them get it ashore. After that, though, Emma and Masterman were able to run the cable around the palm trunks themselves. There was some complicated work involving a lot of pulleys borrowed from the ship, and Emma lost count of all the intricate twists and turns they made. At last Masterman fastened the winch where he wanted it. With a smug smile he began to crank the handle.

Inch by inch, slowly but quite easily, the Grand Wenlocke moved ashore and then up the beach, as though it weighed no more than a rowboat. Captain Doubloon gaped at it, and his parrot laughed.

"That'll teach me," groaned the captain. "Half me treasure's yours, boy."

"Thank you," said Masterman. "Where shall we put the hotel?"

"What about that nice green lawn up there?" suggested Emma, pointing.

When the Grand Wenlocke was where they wanted it at last, Captain Doubloon went around and removed all the cable and empty barrels. The hotel sank into the green grass, but only a little, and then stopped.

"Hurrah!" said Winston, flinging open the doors. "What a beautiful view!"

He got very busy after that, washing the salt spray off the windows and unfastening everything that had been lashed in place while the hotel moved over the rolling waves. Emma and Masterman helped him, while Captain Doubloon and Mrs. Beet went strolling arm in arm, looking for coconuts.

No sooner had they gone off among the trees than a raft came floating up to shore, with a lot of people waving from it. It turned out that the castaways were players from a ballroom orchestra who had been in a shipwreck, and very conveniently saved their instruments — all except for the pianist, who was disconsolate. He brightened up considerably, however, when he learned that the Grand Wenlocke had a piano. He set about tuning it right away, and soon there was music flooding out of the open windows of the Ballroom.

That night there was finally a Grand Ball in the Grand Ballroom to celebrate their safe arrival. Emma was able to wear the splendid pink party gown at last! She came slowly down the stairs in her finery, like a princess in a fairy tale.

As the band played, the beautiful people danced only with one another, sleek elegant ballroom dancing. Mr. Eleutherios and his lady friends, by contrast, danced very wildly, scattering grapes and leaves everywhere, but they had a great deal of fun and their faces became very flushed. The Freets danced a sort of minuet, slow and dignified. The People of the Sands disliked dancing, but sat to one side of the Ballroom with their camels, listening to the music.

Captain Doubloon, resplendent in what looked like an old Navy uniform, bowed very low and invited Mrs. Beet out on the dance floor, where they waltzed in a stately if slightly lopsided fashion. Winston lifted Emma in his arms and danced with her, round and round under the twinkling stars. Masterman watched them awhile, pouting, and at last took Shorty's front paws in his hands and joined the dancing as well.

So the Grand Wenlocke settled into its new location, safe at last. It shone on its green lawn, with the sunlight glinting off its windows. Cruise ships passing by spotted it and put in at once. It was a great success.

Captain Doubloon did indeed propose to Mrs. Beet, and they got married by a missionary, who paddled over in a canoe from a nearby island. Mrs. Doubloon (as she was called now) sent the missionary back with an advertisement for kitchen help to put in his local paper. Soon she was able to hire a large staff to work in the Kitchens with her, so she didn't get so tired or need to sit and put her feet up so often.

On the evening after its Grand Relocation Re-opening, Emma went for a walk by herself.

She wandered out across the lawn behind the hotel, and up the hillside beyond, where a little path zigzagged between the trees. It went up quite a long way. Sometimes there were natural steps made of boulders; sometimes the great branching roots of trees themselves made steps. She climbed under canopies of flowering vines, and through thickets of big flowers like hibiscus, and plumeria, and tiare. They made the night air sweet-scented.

Emma came out in a meadow at the top of the hill, and saw the moon rising over the sea. There was the sleepy sound of the waves rolling in on the beach far below, and the sleepy cry of a night bird somewhere back in the trees.

Emma sighed in happiness and sat down, looking out at the night. She knew she could face down any storm that blew. She had made herself a place in the world. No one but she would sit behind the high desk in the Lobby, handing out keys to the guests who came. She thought that it might be a good idea to learn a few of Mrs. Doubloon's secret recipes too, for a girl never knew when she might need to soothe a band of fearsome pirates by whipping up a steamed pudding with rum sauce.

Below her on its lawn, the Grand Wenlocke was a glory of polished brass and crystal, shining like a golden lantern. The rooms were full of music that drifted out on the night air.

Emma had begun her adventure alone, in terror and noise, blown far away from all she had ever known, and had landed in a lonely place with nothing but broken and forgotten things. Now she had come to this peaceful night, and this beautiful mountain.

It would be nice to say that she looked out and saw a boat approaching, with everyone she had lost in the storm waving to her from its deck; but it wouldn't be true. Sometimes we never get back what we lose.

Emma sat for a long while under the stars, remembering the past. She felt, at last, safe enough to cry a little for the people and things she had lost in the storm. She knew she would cry again, as time went on, whenever she thought about them. She knew she would never forget them, and that their loss would always hurt.

But *she*, Emma, wasn't lost anymore, and she knew that the people she had lost would want her to survive, to be happy, to make a new life of her own. She would grow up into a poised and accomplished young lady, while Masterman was growing into his great-grandfather's suits and becoming a handsome and clever young man. Possibly they would fall in love and get married. Possibly they wouldn't. They would certainly have many more adventures together, whatever Storms blew.

Emma dried her tears. She got up and went back down the hill to her friends.

The End